CODE
OF THE
WEST
SHORT STORIES

CODE OF THE WEST

SHORT STORIES

Keith G. Scott

Library of Congress Control Number: 2020921529

PAPERBACK: 978-1-953791-26-9
EBOOK: 978-1-953791-27-6

Ordering Information:

For orders and inquiries, please contact:
1-888-404-1388
www.goldtouchpress.com
book.orders@goldtouchpress.com

Printed in the United States of America

Keith G Scott@geterdone.54

DEDICATION

TO MY 3 FEMALE MUNCHKINS-LOVE
-GRANDADDIO

CONTENTS

STORY 4
ALWAYS FINISH WHAT YOU START

STORY 5
TALK LESS SAY MORE

STORY 6
WHEN YOU MAKE A PROMISE KEEP IT

STORY 7
REMEMBER SOME THING ARE NOT FOR SALE

STORY 1

LIVE EACH DAY WITH COURAGE

CHAPTER 1

Glen Window bursts into my office looking like he has seen a ghost or worse he wipes the sweat off his forehead with his apron, "Sheriff Bloody Graves Manson and his gang just rode in looking like they was rode hard and out away wet, mean with blood in their eyes, Jason this job ain't worth it resign take Susan and leave. There is no meaner bunch anywhere in the west they will shoot you down like a dog in the street I have to be getting back to the shop, thought should know, now remember what I said run boy, run or die" Glen is the Barber he sees and hears everything I believe he gets pleasure out of passing on bad news the gals snicker and call him a busy body, before I can respond he rushes out of the office so he can spread the word around town-"asshole".

Damn Graves Manson why the hell of all the towns did he have to pick my town to stop in, when Glen mentioned who had come to town I went numb inside with fear, I hope the barber could see it as I try to look calm, never in my life have I felt a fear this strong my mind goes fuzzy and my arms and legs feel weak, I look for the bucket as my stomach sours. My Old man was Ramrod for the huge Angus ranch in Colorado he had fought about everything there is but coffee and pie and survived I can hear him now, "Son everyone gets scared and if they tell you otherwise they are liars or insane being some scared is good sharpens the senses gets the blood flowing but you must control it or it will consume you, deep breaths the calmer you can keep your mind the better chance you will stay alive plenty of time to be scared after it is over. "Never let your enemy know your fear, always stay on the attack, keep them off balance boy if you are going to die with a bullet in your guts go down a wolf not a damn sheep."

I reach into my vest pocket and light up a long thin black Mexican cigar and begin to consider my situation more calmly but no matter what I know I am in the shit, deep, one man against 4 of the most vicious killers anywhere in the west I suspect Al Simpson the owner of the Brass Knuckle Saloon is already taking bets on how long I will survive. Well I will tell you what I aim spoiling their fun but not sure how I am going to do it and not get shot to doll rags, suddenly alarmed I jump to my feet I must find my lovely wife Susan and have her not do her shopping today I dash out hoping to catch her in time. I recon I better introduce myself my name is Jason Flynn I am Deputy Sheriff for the town of Eldorado Oklahoma and county, I just turned 21 and have only been Sheriff for a little over 4 months after long time Sheriff Blazer Adams retired and moved to the oceanside somewhere. The main reason I took this job is I just got married to my beautiful Susan and with wages and tax collecting I make more in wages and work less than a working cowboy but I have done my share of time in the hurricane deck, made three trail drives with Pa between Indians, rivers, rustlers and just bad luck we left a trail of dead cowboys behind us. Eldorado is a small town probably no more than 260 people, as towns go it is typical of most western towns, false front building lining the wide main street, saloon, general store, feed store, the one special thing the town has is its own newspaper run by a young idealist by the name of Horace Du Pont at one end of the street is the Livery and corrals at the other end our small church and graveyard. Outlaws like Bloody Manson sought out small towns on the other side of the Texas border to escape lawman and Rangers, they take what they want and kill or brutalize anyone who gets in their way, I swear to myself no matter what Manson and his thugs are not hazing my town- no fooling.

Susan is just leaving the house when I intercept her, I give her my best smile and a kiss on the check she smells of lavender and fresh baked bread, I inhale deeply loving the smell of her but now the hard part telling Susan I am not sure how she will react when faced with the hard facts, neither one of expected this sort of thing to happen but this is why they pay me the big money. "Susan honey you cannot go shopping and must stay close to the house, Graves Manson are in town and they are a bad bunch not above assaulting and killing women, now honey please come back into the house with me" Susan is quiet as if she speaks the reality of it all will break through I gently take her by the hand and lead her towards the house looking down the street I spy Wildcat Wilson walking towards us using Indian sign language I ask me to join me in the house, he nods in agreement, a stroke of luck.

CHAPTER 2

BLOODY GRAVES MANSON

Bloody Manson stares into his whiskey glass, his mood black as midnight not only did he and his men just barely escaped death or capture, them damn Rangers never let up on a man but to make things worse they only made off with about 200 dollars from the last robbery that is not going to take them far. A small sneer appears on his dirty unshaven face at least they found a good spot to hide out, he and his men will take everything before they move on and that includes the women. Graves now looks around the table at the men he rides with and leads, all like himself covered in trail dust unshaven and looking wore down, these men are the worst of the worse like Lucky Hank Lewis born killer from the Nations, tall, thin long sandy coloured hair to his shoulders, pale almost dead looking eyes, loves to work with a knife and gets his kicks from the screams of his victims, once dead he takes a finger from each unfortunate and keeps them in a leather sack, one sick bastard.

Barndoor Blaine looks like a small mountain sitting beside Lucky Lewis his ham sized hands to big for a revolver so he carries a double barrelled 12 gauge shotgun in a holster tied to his right thigh, the left side of his gun belt holds a saber with a broken blade near 20 inches long and sharpened to a needle point, Graves has seen Barndoor slice a mans head clean off with one powerful stroke, not much on smarts but good man to have when muscle or intimidation is needed. The last member of his gang is Silent Sam Bundy, Sam is a mystery he don't talk much cause his drunken Pa chocked him as a boy so hard he damaged Sam's voice box making it difficult to speak, being raised mean made Sam even meaner, everything about Sam was dark always dressed in black, he is one of the rare 2 gun rig gunfighters his black gun belt he carries 2 black handled .45 colt revolvers with the front sights shaved off, Sam may be quiet but he talks big and loud with his six guns, grease lightning with either hand.

Graves looks to his men he distrusts and is disgusted by them all but they do their work well and with Graves its all about money booze and women especially young women, after they kill that kid Sheriff the towns people will crumble and he will take every damn thing they have and leave this shit hole of a town burning behind them after he and the boys have had their fun. For now Graves is content to wait, good bonded whiskey and decent food, that young fool Sheriff should be along soon to bad for him he will be dragged out by the heels leaving behind a big blood trail the boys tend to get bloody especially with lawmen.

Wildcat Wilson has seen more than 50 summers come and go and knows at once there must be trouble if the young Sheriff Jason Flynn is using Indian sign and wanting to meet in secret, Wildcat smiles about damn time there is some excitement damn west is getting way to civilized and populated to his liking, making sure no one is watching he slips in the back door of Jason's small house. He is greeted with worried smiles by both husband and wife Wildcat removes his old brown floppy hat and nods to Susan, you would not know to look at him but he had a classical education and upbringing in old Virginia and his dear mother was a stickler for manners, "Howdy Jason, Ma'am how y'all doing today, you 2 look like you just seen a hoard of blood thirsty Apaches are coming for your scalps, now Susan how about you heat up the coffee and Jason you can tell me what's going on old Wildcat is here to help."

Damn am I pleased to see the frontiersman now I have a sliver of hope for here is a mountain of a mountain man, iron on iron hard, sly as a fox and the courage of the wolf, I know now at least Susan will be safe as long as he draws a breath, a man who will live and die by the code, Susan brings the coffee to the table and joins us I fill Wildcat in. "Well old friend I recon I would rather face them Apaches Bloody Graves Mason and his gang are in town and now drinking it up in the Cactus Rose saloon, no need to tell either one of you what they plan to do, if I cannot stop them people and the town will die if nothing else Graves keeps things simple kill and take what he wants." Wildcat I will be obliged if you can do 2 things for me, first I need you to send a telegraph to the Arizona Rangers about Graves and his gang and ask them to come a running but need to do it quick they will figure to cut the wires soon, and I would like your word you will be Susan's protector, I know of no other man I trust more with my most precious possession. "Now I have to be getting back to the Sheriffs office show myself I do not want people think I am hiding or running scared, can I count on you Hoss?" There really was no need to ask the man is of the old breed where you stuck by your friends thick or thin, and offering protection to a lady is not only a duty but a privilege, and he was not so much about law as about justice basic right and wrong, a good way common sense can go a long way. I ask Susan not to leave the house for any reason then strap my gun belt on and head for the door I notice to my shame my hand shaking slightly as I grab the door handle, taking a deep breath then step out into the street.

A duck on water, I deliberately walk down the middle of the main street my walk steady and confident my face a blank mask, inside the fear begins to chew on my guts, my aim is for the towns people to see their Sheriff has not deserted them, but most people stop and stare I get the feeling they are looking at a dead Sheriff who has just not fallen down yet. It is a damn long walk down the short wide street but I finally make it to my office out of prying eyes I remove my Stetson and wipe the sweat from my forehead once seated behind my desk I light up a cigar and start to think all I know is I ain't running. Long since is the snot nosed wet behind the ears kid they think they are facing will take a couple with me before they put me under. The cigar tastes bitter, there comes times in a mans life where they just have say the hell with it and go, standing I remove my gun belt and hang it on a peg, before I can change my mind I leave the office and head to the saloon about time Graves and I got acquainted, I know I am taking a big gamble but Pa always told me when you get in a tight spot do the unexpected, going into the killers lair unharmed will hopefully lead them to believe I have a trap set, hell of a bluff.

There is not hesitation I do not stop at the saloon batwing doors with a quick glance and find Bloody and his men seems the gang has grown there are now six dirty looking hardcases sitting together around a couple tables pushed together, "shit", walking towards their table I keep my hands in plain sight I spot Manson right off we lock eyes he does look a bit surprised hoping my voice comes out steady I begin to lay it out for them.

Mr Manson my name is Jason Flynn I am Sheriff here for Eldorado town and county and these are my words, pay heed, you ain't treeing my town you will enjoy the day getting drunk, eating and resting up but you will all be gone by noon tomorrow or I will jail you or if I am forced to kill you, you go find another town to prey on you will find Eldorado hard chewing, have I made myself clear Manson?" Graves smiles to himself he could not help but admire the young Sheriff for his brass, took sand to walk in unarmed, but it was stupid he will not leave the saloon alive. "Sheriff you got the balls the size of a brahma bull coming in here and ordering us around maybe you failed at your sums in school but as I see it there are 6 of us and one of you I don't recon you will get much help from the town sheep, but no uppity Deputy Sheriff is going to tell me what to do, we will do as we please you should have stuck to punching cows boy cause you are not leaving this saloon alive."

To my surprise I smile at the killer and his men my fear gone for the moment, "Graves you talk big with 5 thugs behind you, as you can see I came in unarmed, I did this for 2 reasons, first I am good but no man can beat this number of guns, and second and this is the important part boys, it is one thing to shoot down an armed lawman, but to kill one that is unarmed and making talk is another you kill me every Lawman and bounty hunter in Texas and Arizona will be hunting you, there will be no peace it will live in constant fear exhaustion and in time welcome death, I would give it some thought Graves." Damn this Sheriff if they kill him now every damn law dog will be on their trail never stopping well he can wait they will have to wait take down the young Sheriff out tomorrow, "Alright Sheriff I hear you and we can wait we got all sorts of time and good whiskey but mark my words boy you die in the street tomorrow I am going to gut shoot you rip your guts out and tie them to a stick for the dogs to eat, be seeing you tomorrow Sheriff Flynn."

With a nod I turn and slowly walk out of the saloon I cross the street bee lining for my office, once again alone and out of sight my knees nearly buckle and I feel I may be sick, focusing best I can I put coffee on to heat, I am beginning to feel better, sipping the hot black brew I still cannot believe I pulled that off, but the reality is that when I fight these men tomorrow I do not have a hope in hell, but one thing sure I am putting hot lead into Manson before I go down- sure as shooting.

CHAPTER 3

A LONG ASS DAY

Finishing my coffee I sling my gun belt around my waste and exit the office, I am going to visit all the shops and advise them to stay home and off the streets tomorrow, bullets do not care who they kill and I expect lots of hot lead and gun smoke in the air tomorrow, as expected I got a many good lucks and praise but no offers for help, the west is changing in Pa's day most town men were fighters ex soldiers wilderness men, by now Manson and his men would be hanging with tight ropes around their necks. Eldorado is not a big town so it did not take long to deliver my message now getting close to supper time and I find I am so hungry I could eat a horse hoofs and all, time to go home to my darling Susan and see how old Wildcat made out, I don't recon no help will come in time but maybe they can get the hunt started faster to rid Arizona of these mad dog killers.

Well nothing more can be done today, most folks will be staying close to home with doors locked, a few punks and wanna be bad men will be in the saloon buying the infamous gang drinks, should be no trouble tonight everyone seems happy to wait until tomorrow and see how this human drama plays out, the hell with it I am going home to see my sweet Susan. Wildcat is sitting at the kitchen table sipping coffee, Susan was frying up supper as I enter I see Wildcats hand reach for the huge colt dragoon he had placed on the table, that is one huge gun looks like it should have wheels, when he sees it is me he relaxes and goes back to his coffee. Walking up behind Susan I wrap my arms around her and hug her close and kiss her on the check, her voice is filled with emotion when she tells me to grab a coffee supper will be ready soon, filling my cup and join him at the table. "Jason word has already spread around town of that dumbass stunt you pulled in the saloon, I can't believe old Manson and the boys did not shoot you to doll rags, but smart lad the one thing they did not expect, it buys you time and as long as there as there is breath in your lungs there is hope, I sent out a telegram asking any Rangers in the area to come running and I marked it urgent, now we got to hope we get lucky. "After supper I am going out to keep an eye on things I don't recon them villian's will do anything tonight but drinking and whoring, I hope they go whole hog make them dull and shaky tomorrow, look for every edge in a scrap I will meet you in your office tomorrow and we will see what Graves and his men are made of, justice above all Sheriff we shall smite them a mighty blow show them what real fighting men are made of."

I cannot help but smile at the Mountain mans words he makes it sound like we are going to church instead of facing 6 ruthless killers, "Wildcat I am much obliged to you for helping out and looking after Susan for me no man I trust or respect more except maybe Pa, but it ain't your fight and you better think over carefully what your asking but if you get to the jail first get the coffee brewing got it aged about 3 days now near perfect." Susan went all out with supper the steaks were bigger than the plates, thick and juicy, with a fresh apple pie for dessert, my gal sure can cook and not only in the kitchen, I cannot help thinking is this how a condemned man feels eating his last meal, damn you to hell Bloody Graves Manson. Wildcat says his goodnights and thanks Susan for supper and tells me to sleep sound he will be keeping an eye on the place and he will have the coffee ready.

Susan is doing the supper dishes when out of nowhere she lashes out shaking and crying, "Jason Flynn you are a fool if you think this towns people will appreciate you dying for them, they will plant you and bring in another young man to be slaughtered, Honey lets leave tonight go somewhere where the answer to every problem is solved with a gun. "Jason we must go those men will kill you and I do not to live if you are no longer with me, please Honey for me hitch up the wagon we can be away in an hour." I pull my love close and wrap my arms around her she buries her face in my chest I can feel her hot tears wetting my shirt, I hold tight and kiss her on the forehead, "Love of my life I want to run I want to hide I ask why me why here, but honey you know I can't and won't I would rather die in the street with lead in my guts than be branded a coward, Pa lived by the code and always said- A MAN NEEDS TO LIVE EACH DAY WITH COURAGE, now I know what that means, but Susan don't count me dead yet, this ain't my first gun battle and I ain't easy to kill, Because I have you and not Manson or any other son of a bitch is going to keep me from you, now honey leave everything and come to bed I need you in my arms tonight."

Never have I had a longer or more difficult night, my body is weary but my mind will not stop, there is no fear like 3 in the morning fear where you are at your weakest, cold sweat escapes my pores, I pray to every God I ever heard of can't do no harm, some calm returns morning is coming weather I like it or not, I imagine men all throughout time who have had to fight have felt this way scared and feeling very alone, these men saddled up and got er done, I aim to do the same just have not figured out how to not end up dead. Frustrated I gently crawl out of bed not to wake Susan, grabbing my clothes I leave the bedroom and dress in the kitchen, it is still full dark so I light a lamp and get the coffee heating, while the coffee heats I fetch my gun cleaning kit gun belt and my short barreled colt .45 revolver belly gun, then take my .45 Schofield out of its leather holster, ike any other tool guns needs caring for you take care of them they will not let you down, sipping my coffee I unload both the Schofield and .45 colt and start breaking them down.

Susan had no better night she comes out of the bedroom putting on her house coat pours herself a coffee then sits quiet watching me clean and oil my tools of pain blood and death, we both remain quiet as if our voices will shatter the calm and having reality flooding in, he coffee finished she gets up and goes into the kitchen to fix up some breakfast. Satisfied I re assemble both revolvers and place fresh shells in each, looking out the kitchen window I see the eastern sky turning pink and hear the morning birds are greeting the day, any other morning it gives me pleasure to greet the day that wonderful moment of peace before the world wakes up, I surely hope this ain't my last sunrise.

CHAPTER 4

GUN TALK

Susan and I talk quietly over breakfast both avoiding any conversation of the challenge and scrap to come, she looks so beautiful in the morning light I can only describe it as she makes my heart sing and strength to do what needs doing. It is nearly full light almost time to head to the jail one more coffee and cigar then I have to leave, it is going to be difficult to leave my lovely wife this morning, we sit together holding hands, I know she hates what I have to do but being western knows this is the only way. It is now or never I stand strap on my gun belt tying the holster to my leg, the .45 colt I stick in my belt for a quick draw, Susan hugs and kisses me before I leave she tells me, "Jason Flynn I want you to know I am proud to be your wife and companion, you be iron on iron hard today, if you die you die a wolf, but I say you will not die today, Honey kill every one of those son of a bitches, I love you."

Afraid I may get teared up I rush from the house then take a moment to collect myself then begin my walk to the jail, so much for telling people to stay home the sides of the street is filled with onlookers to witness history and stories to tell their Grandkids, well I warned them I got my own problems at the moment. Entering my office I am surprised to see Wildcat talking to a stranger they look up from their coffee, Wildcat hurries to make the introductions, "Jason, I mean Sheriff Flynn this here is a friend of mine and the best damn lawman in Arizona, Jason meet Ranger Regret Cooper, most folks know him as the Stormrider, he has come to lend a hand." The tall Ranger stands and we shake hands, I can feel the strength within the man as if some unseen force, his chiselled jaw is unshaven, but it his is eyes dark and hard, some folks say he is part Indian and has old magic that he can read a mans soul, but his smile is right friendly and I will say I am damn glad he is here, I might just survive the day.

The tall Ranger helps himself to another coffee and strikes a match to his cigar before speaking, "Pleasure to meet you Jason old Wildcat here has been telling me about Bloody Manson and the situation here, luckily I was just down the road a bit in Bitter Creek finishing some work when word came through the wires, figured I would mosey over this old coot here always did like hogging all the fun. "I believe I got into town unseen I got Storm in your corral out back so no one knows I am here, and we will keep it that way give Graves and his boys a surprise. "Sheriff you have to be wang leather strong today, this fight coming up is kill or be killed I aim for this to be the end of the trail for Manson and is gang of polecats, we are not giving quarter when this scrap is over every one of those son of a bitches will be dead in the street, Arizona will have no more of their evil ways. "Now if you boys care to hear it I have a plan to take those boys down, and if you can think of anything better I more than willing to listen but I can see no way where we might have to eat some lead, these are no ordinary outlaws they are mad dog killers, tough and damn dangerous, make every shot a kill shot, now here is what I recon we should do."

The Stormrider's words rang true, I think to myself how calm these men seem with death waiting up the street, both looking cool as a mountain stream, they say experience is the best teacher I know both men are survivors of many battles can it be they no longer have fear. Death rides is on their shoulders and they know it and do not give a shit they know the rule on men who use guns. The plan is simple and I surely could not think of any better plan, without realizing it I begin to pace back and forth across the office my new deputies notice how I am on edge and a bit jumpy, the Ranger breaks the silence. "Sheriff come sit down and have a cigar, Jason I was very lucky when Buck took me under his wing, one thing he taught me is every man is scared before a battle if they say they are not they are either liars or insane, it is not so much about the fear as how you deal with it, you must embrace it, it sharpens the senses and reflexes believe me Mr. Flynn you are not the only man afraid in this room, no shame in it at all." Wildcat backed up the Rangers words my mind calms one thing I know that if I die today I will be fighting on the side of law and order and having the best of the best at my side, my biggest fear about dying is what will become of Susan, I push it from my mind, no time for this now.

The wall clock chimes time to go to work I stand to get myself ready, the Ranger passes on a last bit of advise, "Sheriff you and Wildcat each grab yourself a greener a lawman's best friend is a sawed off 12 gauge. Friend of mine swears by them you might of heard of him United States Marshal Sudden Steele, made me a believer, the Canadian gunfighter Seth Bullock once back down a lynch mob up Montana way with nothing but a shotgun and guts, men may buck a six gun but a shotgun will give them pause every damn time. "Now when I let loose you boys pull both triggers drop the gun and go to your sidearms, once the shooting starts he hit them hard and keep hitting until every last one is down and out, better to shoot straight than fast old Buck used to say, ok Jason time to get er done, good luck." I shake hands with my 2 hero's before I step out into the middle of the street alone hoping my voice does not fail me, I call out my challenge to my enemies.

"Manson you dirty son of a bitch this is Sheriff Flynn your time is up and you have had your warning, now come out and face me you yellow livered piece of shit," well that gets their attention I can hear cursing and rough threats coming from the saloon, I grip the shotgun tightly my hands are sweaty my mouth dry as I wait for a pissed off outlaw leader and his thugs to come out. The batwing doors slam open and 6 outlaws emerge they enter the street lining up beside one another like a human wall. I know Manson would want to make his brag before killing me so I wait it does not take long, "Damn Sheriff if you ain't the one, well kid you got sand but you ain't the sharpest stick in the pile and I warned you what I will do, you have to die slow and hard as an example to the sheep of the town, damn shame really, none of these people really care you are going to die alone on this dusty street well time to get to it boy." I see Graves and his men reading themselves to draw just then the Stormrider and Wildcat come out of the office and stand by my side.

"Manson I may get myself killed today but I will not die alone but with real fighting men standing beside me, I would like you boys to meet Wildcat Wilson who has killed more men than the plaque and Arizona Ranger Regret Cooper or better known as the Stormrider you might of heard of him, now lets get to fighting you will be dining with the devil tonight." I step off 3 across we walk towards the gang, shotguns ready, Manson's men are now looking confused and scared both my comrades are known to them as bad men to cross then with out warning the Ranger cuts loose with his shotgun, Wildcat and I a split second later, I let the shotgun go and draw my belly gun I feel it bucking in my hand. This is where the Schofield does its deadly work, the .45 hits like a mule kick and you hit them they stay down.

Graves cannot believe what's happening it is like a nightmare he cannot wake from, the damn Stormrider of all people 2 off his men are downed by the shotguns, Lucky is wounded and fighting from the ground, a chuck of hot lead smashes into his left shoulder spinning him around he drops his empty revolver and grabs up his spare, damn that kid Sheriff. Barndoor had been hit by some of big lead shotgun pellets but they had little effect pulling his deadly broken sword he focuses on Wildcat, the old mountain man sees the brute coming for him and smiles as he pulls his Arkansas toothpick from its sheath, Barndoor charges and takes a mighty swipe at Wildcats belly, the Mountain man easily avoids the rush and gives his big enemy a slash across his back for his mistake. Poor old Barndoor picked the wrong man to fight with cold steel, in his youth Wilson was taught fencing later on in life he learned his knife fighting by a Mexican master and by his Indian friends and enemies. Barndoor is a bloody mess bleeding out from more than 20 deep cuts, tiring of the game Wildcat feints to his left the big man responds opening his neck and throat, the big outlaw dies as the big knife slices open his throat it was an ugly death most deserving.

The gunfire stops in the screaming silence Manson sees he is the only one left alive he braces himself for the impact of lead striking him but none comes, I look to the Ranger, "if it is all the same to you Ranger Manson is my meat, I recon he started it only fitting I end it, he threatened to take my life and I did not much care for that, you know a man has to saddle his own broncs out here to survive." The Ranger smiles and has no problem at all with me taking Manson, looking to Wildcat he looks fearsome covered in Barndoors blood, I call out to Graves. "Manson step out and meet me just you and me, lets see if your shooting iron is as fast as your mouth, the boys here will stay out of it, now let's open the ball."

Manson can not believe his luck he will get to kill this punk law dog, and he will still gut shoot the bastard and watch him squirm, he takes a couple steps forward then his hand flashes down grabbing his smoke wagon, just as his gun was coming out of its holster he is hit twice in the chest by heavy lead bullets which smash and shatter his bones then shred his lungs, with a look of surprise his gun falls from his dead fingers his knees buckle and falls on his face in the dirt, a fitting end for a rabid dog.

I look around at the carnage I am sickened by it, but I will tell you what I am damn happy to still be alive, like gophers the towns people start popping out of there holes now the danger has past, I turn and see my sweet Susan running towards me I take a step towards her but something seems wrong with my leg it gives out and I go down on my other knee, damn I think igot myself shot. The bullet hit me in the fleshy part of my calf just below the knee, now that is see it the pain hits, one thing I learned is getting shot hurts and I don't plan on making a habit of it. Wildcat and Regret carry me to the Doctors office Regret tells me I done real good and he will write up the report I should just tend to my leg and my beautiful wife, the mountain man said he will get the bodies buried boot hill and look after things until I am up and moving.

I heard once a brave man only dies once where a coward dies many deaths, after today I am a believer.

-YOU WILL NEVER DO ANYTHING IN THIS WORLD WITHOUT COUAGE. IT IS THE GREATEST QUALITY OF THE MIND NEXT TO HONOR- ARISTOTLE

STORY 2

TAKE PRIDE IN YOUR WORK

CHAPTER 1

1ST SGT. MORGAN PRICE

Fort Riley is one hell of a desolate spot located in Kansas near the Republic River country I survey the landscape the hugeness and openness of land and sky is almost overwhelming as if you are adrift on an ocean of grass, I can count the trees on one hand and have fingers left over, down by the river it is nicer but I learned a long time back them who decides where to put forts are pure dumbasses. My name is Sgt. Bren Donovan of the famous 5th Cavalry the Black Knights I am one of two Sgt's assigned to the Indian scouts the other is 1st Sgt Morgan Pryce who in my opinion is the best damn Sgt in the 5th this is my story and I am sticking to it.

Morgan and I first hooked up during the late war fighting with Major General John Buford, Pryce was a Captain and myself his Sgt., the Captains unit was the pride of the outfit first into the scrap last out, we were known as Pryce's Pirates. Capt. Pryce was decorated for bravery twice once for saving the Generals life at the battle of Gettysburg, I swear the man has ice in his veins, wounded 4 times just to come back meaner than ever myself suffered a musket ball through the leg and a bayonet in the side the Pirates always had a bit of strut for to get into Pryce's outfit you had to prove yourself first, damn we had some scraps.

When the horrors of the war ceased the military had to many men so to stay you were reduced in rank but the Indian wars were beginning and they needed fighting men to head west to protect settlers and the railroad builders, Pryce and I don't know much except fighting so we hooked up with the 5th Cavalry Morgan as a 1st Sgt and me a Cpl but now promoted to Sgt., today home is Fort Riley Kansas and our duty is to work with the Indian scouts. Many officers and NCO's look upon the unit with contempt and distrust in their narrow minds and Indian is just a damn Indian, but not Pryce he went right to the commanding officer and volunteered us one thing Morgan is very good at is spotting fighting men and he knew these Navajo Scouts were warriors and wolves, next thing I know I am moving our kit over to where they house the scouts- "damn Sgts".

The Scouts are assigned 2 officers the Commander is Capt. John Hook and a shave tail Lt. out of West Point a very wet behind the ears Lt. Ian Mallory. Capt. Hook is a narrow minded by the book officer who feels he has been slighted by being assigned to lead the scouts the Capt. does not much like or trust anyone not white, a real asshole. Both Morgan and I knew Lt. Mallory's father Sgt Major Duke Mallory, a fine man and deadly warrior, Ian got into West Point because his father won the Medal OF Honor but sadly died in the last months of the war, if he is anything like his old man he will do right fine if not Morgan and I will whip him into shape.

There are 6 Navajo Scouts in the unit, all experienced warriors the best of the best the leaders of the scouts are brothers Tse which means "Rock" and his younger brother Ahiga which means "he who fights" and their names fit them to a T, Tse is quiet thoughtful listens more and talks less, iron on iron hard like his name implies but he can track a skeeter through a rainstorm and is one hell of a fighter. Ahiga is a man who lets his brother do the thinking he just wants to hunt his prey and be the first into the fight, damn good men all.

Morgan knows what he is in for and thrives off the challenges the 1st Sgt. Knows he can learn much from these scouts which he in turn will pass on to others making the Regiment better and maybe saving soldiers lives. The 1st Sgt. Knows you cannot treat the scouts like soldiers and ignores the interesting mixture of Navajo and military uniform but insists on a morning parade to check weapons, horses and equipment as for ourselves we will be sharply dressed in garrison, Morgan is a man who has always taken pride in the uniform he wears and sets an example for all Nco's to follow. I am just heading to chow when the 1st Sgt. Hunts me down and says the Capt. wants to see us pronto, why in holy hell do officers always call meeting when it is time for chow and coffee, taking a quick check of my uniform I follow along behind Morgan orders are orders.

CHAPTER 2

THE PATROL

We enter the Captains office and come to attention in front of his desk, with a wave he tells us to stand easy, the Lt. is also in the office and looking a might uncomfortable, the Capt. lights a cheap cigar before we receive our orders. "Lt Mallory you will take a patrol to include the Sgts and all the scouts to search out and find the enemy, we know they are mostly Arapaho with some Sioux led by a new leader by the name of Little Raven, you are not to engage your job is to find them and give us some idea of the number of hostiles we face, this is from the Commanding Officer himself, it is vital you find them and report back, more homesteaders are being burned out and killed every day, you will leave at first light if there are no questions you men are dismissed." There are none we salute and depart the Captains office, Morgan informs the Lt that we are going for chow and coffee and requests a meeting with the scouts in an hour at the corrals, there is much to do.

By the time we get to the chow hall most of the troops have eaten and are back doing their assigned duties, we fill our trays with beans bread and some form of meat grab a coffee and join Sgt Major Irons at his table and fill him in on our meeting with the Capt. The Sgt Major is pure Cavalry been in the outfit since he was between to grass and the hay, a man of rare common sense and intellect, tough but fair you do as your told and behave there is never a problem he will come down on you like a landslide and has not problem giving out punishments, may not be overly liked but he more importantly is respected as a outstanding soldier, "Boys you be damn careful there are many hostiles riding the plains with war paint and knives running red with homesteaders blood, this villain Little Raven has had a few minor victories and warriors are beginning to believe it is time for war, I don't have to tell you boys to keep an eye on young Lt. Mallory, like you boys I knew his old man, hell of a soldier. "Now lads you did not here it from me the General himself will be coming out to lead the Regiment on the upcoming campaign and you know what a stickler he is for good intelligence, no damn heroics either get in see what you can find out and haul ass back, the longer this thing goes the much innocent blood will be spilled, well boys got to run good luck, have fun and get er done."

The Navajo scouts and Lt, Mallory are already at the corrals waiting when we arrive, Pryce produces a sack of tobacco and papers and hands it to the scouts then greats them in their language, the scouts trust and respect the 1stSgt. like most Indian tribes the Navajo respect courage and a fighting man above all else and like anyone else who knows the big lunkhead is hell on wheels warrior. Once the smokes and cigars are going Morgan tells the scout they are going on the hunt and the Lt. will give the briefing, most of the scouts spoke good English so there is no need for a translator, the Lt. does a good job briefing, no bullshit, short and to the point I can see Pryce smile a touch on the young officers conduct, when finished he asks for questions, this is second nature to the scouts they know more what to do than we do, before dismissing Pryce addresses Lt. Mallory, "Sir if you do not mind a suggestion I believe we leave earlier than first light if I was Little Raven I would have warriors watching the fort, I think we should sneak out at about 4 while still full dark and Sir if you have a few minutes the Sgt and myself would appreciate a few private words." Without hesitation the Lt. agrees with both suggestions the scouts go about their duties and we 3 hunt some shade to sit and talk a spell.

Morgan looks over at the young man his grin huge," Ian lad last time Bren and I saw you were knee high to a grasshopper you have grown tall and strong and you do well filling out the uniform, now I cannot answer for the officers but you will have no problem with the NCO's most still remember your Dad the Sgt Major, hell the lot of us would have followed him into the 7th level of hell, now my boy tell why you joined the scouts this is a volunteer position for junior officers most young officers would shun it even look down on it". The Lt smiles at us, "Growing up Pa always wanted me to be an officer the first in the new country, he always told me when I get to my first duty assignment I should find the best Sgt. and learn from him long enough to get to know how to stay alive and more important to keep my men alive. "He always said you two men were the best of the best so here I am, now for the fellow officers I have done my share of knuckle and skull and have no problem bruising my knuckles, men I will be looking to you for guidance but the final decisions are mine, is that understood Sgt's?" We both smile give him some mock salutes and separate to get ourselves ready for travel walking away Pryce looks to me, "Bren me bucko I do believe we may finally have a young shavetail with some potential well we better get to it see you for supper."

The 1st Sgt and I are old hands at this and most of our kit was ready to go all I really needed was an extra canteen and ammunition we will be pretty well armed if we meet trouble, the scouts have been given .45 70 Sharps rifles and carried their own personal weapons, the 1st Sgt and I both carried 44.40 Winchester rifles, .44 caliber colt revolvers and 12 gauge sawed of shotguns are hidden until out of sight, those short cannons are damn effective for close quarter fighting. Pryce and myself have both grown fond of the thin black Mexican cigars picked the habit up when we were working along the Mexican border, knowing the 1st Sgt would forget I wander over to

Fowlers Emporium and pick up a box of cigars and a large bag of buffalo jerky, with enough water a man can survive a long while on jerky and cigars, I return to my bunk with my packages and rest a few minutes before heading over for supper.

Morgan and the Sgt Major are already eating when I join them with my tray filled with beef stew and biscuits, I plan on eating hardy this will probably be the last hot meal for some time, a fire at night on the grassy plains can be seen a long way and it is likely to bring unwanted company, the 1st Sgt is telling the Sgt Major about our meeting with the Lt. and figures with experience will make a good officer, I throw in my 2 bits worth agreeing with Pryce. In our misguided youth we were both fond of the bottle and as every good NCO did some time in the Guardhouse and now only on rare occasions do we hit the hootch, tonight after supper we agreed we should treat ourselves to a couple beers over at the Regiment canteen then early to the rack. Entering the canteen Pryce grabs a table and grab a couple of cold beers from the bar and join him, passing him a cigar we light up and settle in to enjoy the moment, sadly it is short lived.

Sgt Baines is a brute of a man huge powerful and loves to use his rank and power to intimidate, he also is a narrow minded asshole who hates most everything including Indians and in his small mind they are all the same and should be wiped out, he has put away a fair amount of what they pass for whiskey out here and is feeling mean and the need to hurt someone, he smiles as his eyes lock on the 1st Sgt. He hates Pryce because he got him busted back to Trooper once and did time in the hoosegow, with a leer he heads towards where we are sitting, I smile to myself at how stupid some people can be, this should be fun.

Pryce watches calmly as the behemoth approaches then I see that glint in his eye and a small smile appear on his face Pryce Morgan is a fighter and loves it, the tougher the better the big man stands before us his hands on his hips and in a taunting voice begins to goad Pryce, "Well looky boys here is the Red N****R lover and his ass kissing Sgt., damn you stinking up the place I can smell dirty Indian on both of you, one of these days soon 1st Sgt I am going to catch you alone and I will break your back before killing you, I say what I mean." 1st Sgt Pryce looks to me and shrugs then turns his attention his attention back to Sgt Baines, "Sgt you are a shame to the Regiment if I had my way I would have you busted out you do not deserve to wear the uniform you are a disgrace and below pondscum, now big mouth time to see if you are as tough as you talk, soldiers fight 20 minutes behind the corrals", with that we get up and leave the bar Sgt. Baines is about to learn a painful lesson, I am going to enjoy it very much.

Pryce is not only a warrior he is highly trained in the skills of hand to hand combat, his Father was a hard man and the master of a merchant ship out of Cardiff Wales, Pryce went to sea the first time by the time he was 11, Pryce was born a fighter and in his worldly travels would get anyone who he could to teach him different fighting skills, in his growing years he had sea mates teach him boxing, wrestling some fancy type of Chinese fighting and every dirty trick in a down and dirty knuckle and skull bust up. Besides his fighting skills Pryce was iron on iron hard and had the strength and power of is ancestors the Celtic warriors. Before going to the stables we swing by the NCO quarters where Pryce takes off his tunic now only in a white undershirt and puts on a pair of skin tight leather gloves with us leaving the fort in mere hours he cannot risk breaking his hands with a hazardous patrol starting in a few hours but the challenge has been made and Morgan Pryce never in his live backed away from a good scrap.

The bruiser and his cronies are waiting I don't trust any of them and got my .44 revolver tucked in my belt behind my back I have been covering Morgan's back now more years than I care to remember he is to much a soldier and wolf to be put under by some backshooting polecat plus I do enjoy watching him work. Sgt Baines is once again flapping his gums with taunts and threats near insane with the lust for blood spittle coming from the corners of his mouth. I give my friend a pat of the shoulder, "Morgan my lad he is surely a big brute and you know he will kill you if he can so I advise taking him out quick he hits you with a haymaker you could land in the next county, well Pard have fun and get er done we leave in camp in

3 hours". The 1st Sgt gives me one of his big grins and walks out to meet his opponent, with the toe of his boot he draws a line in the dirt and looks at the human mountain, "Alright asshole come get some."

With a growl the big Sgt. Charges hoping to catch Morgan and put him on the ground where his size will give him the advantage Morgan shifts his feet and as the big man gets close Morgan grabs his arm and using a hip throw tosses the big man in the air and finding gravity is a bitch when the wind is knocked out of him, Morgan could finish the brute right here but this is no longer a fight but a brutal and painful lesson with Sgt Baines as the student. Morgan waits as the big man recovers on his feet now Baines is wary and comes in close to hammer Pryce with his ham sized fists, suddenly Bains lets go with a roundhouse punch at Morgan's head, a powerful swing that could have knocked down a bull moose but being a brawler and not a fighter he telegraphed the punch I think Morgan saw it coming from a mile back he easily goes under the punch and makes Baines pay with a him with a hard left hand to the ribs, I hear the sound of ribs cracking Baines grunts with pain but now he is black mad and attacks once more, this time Morgan delivers a vicious kidney shot making the big man scream in pain, now most men would just pick him apart looking for an opening for the right punch but not my knot head stubborn Pard always has to prove himself the better man he laughs at the brute and takes his stance. Sgt Baines cannot believe his luck Pryce the asshole is willing to stand toe to toe and slug it out, what a fool. Both men come together and almost shoulder to shoulder begin to deliver punches heavy blows both men determined not to take a step back until Pryce catches Baines with a hard blow to the mans injured ribs the big Sgt takes his first step back, then it was just brutal Pryce just beat the crap out of Baines, hitting him hard and fast with both hands the fight ends suddenly when Morgan lands a beautiful uppercut to the big mans chin, with a step back the defeated mans eyes roll back in his head and does not feel his nose being smashed when he falls face first to the hard packed ground.

Everything goes quiet, Bains Cronies look at the their fallen champion not believing not only that be got beat but how easy 1st

Sgt Pryce took him apart, I see a weaselly looking Trooper is slowly moving his hand to his unflapped holster I pull my revolver and pull the hammer back, the sound is loud in the night I may not be famous like my friend but I am known as a fighter in the Regiment and I do not bluff and will kill if provoked. The trooper wisely moves his hand away from his sidearm I tell Sgt Bains bunch to get the man to the base hospital and I strongly encourage them to move quickly I watch until I feel it is safe and hurry to join him, his legend would grow once again after tonight there are few kept secrets in the military.

The guard quietly opens the forts main gate just wide enough for us to get through leading our horses and moving quiet we sneak out into the dark night Tse and Morgan are the forward scouts, I am tired and a bit peckish but despite the danger I am happy to be out of the fort I am much more at ease in the wilds, I already know one thing we got to be fox smart and wang leather strong if we do not want our scalps hanging from some warriors coup stick or spear.

CHAPTER 3

WARRIORS MEET

We walk our horses for about an hour before mounting up, before Tse and the 1st Sgt head forward he tells the Lt. they will meet again at Shadow Spring near the breaks to water the horses and have a quick noon for coffee and chow, I ride up to join the Lt., "A very good day to you Sir no worries we will just head east the scouts and myself know where the Sgt wants to meet and a good spot but I am just reminding the Lt. there could be unwanted company waiting we will have to approach slow and careful, out here water always means life but it also brings death. "Looking over the young lad I notice he is not carrying a knife, I reach into my saddlebag and retrieve my spare knife a wicked nasty looking Arkansas toothpick about 14 inches in total secured in a beautiful leather sheath a Navajo gal made me, I hand it to the young officer. "Lad when we noon strap that to your belt, this is your last line of defence and even in the age of guns many times it comes down to cold steel to survive, and Sir that knife is hair splitting sharp, I heard Bat Masterson say one time "Run towards a gun and away from a knife." The young officer accepts the knife and words with his thanks, I know if Morgan and I can keep him alive until he gets some time in the saddle he will make a fine officer which in my humble opinion we are sorely lacking in the outfit. Looking forward I can see our destination I pull my rifle from its boot and make sure there is a round up the tube all the scouts have their Spencer rifles out Ahiga moves into the lead with all eyes searching the grassy landscape we follow.

To my great delight as we near the meeting place I can see Sgt Pryce and Tse are already there and waiting with coffee brewing over a near smokeless fire in the shade of heavily leaved trees, relaxing now we ride in and leaving the saddles we loosen the cinches on then water and picket the horses in the shade before joining Morgan and Tse for some hot black life giving coffee. Tse sends one of his scouts to keep a lookout while we eat and talk over out next move. Tse tells us they spotted many unshod horses tracks separate bunches numbering from as few as 6 and as large as 20, but they all seem to be heading in the same general direction the signs are clear the villain Little Raven is bringing his warriors together I believe this war chief has big plans but who knows what that sly Arapaho has on his mind. Both Morgan and Tse believe the best bet is that he is bringing them to the Valley of the Ancient Stones use the site and its magic to convince his followers his magic is strong, he will tell the warriors through his visions from the other side that if they fight strong and without mercy they will once again ride free in the oceans of grass once again.

Finishing my coffee and a couple old biscuits I light up a cigar and grab my long gun to go relieve the scout on watch to make sure he gets time to eat and have coffee the 1st Sgt does not like long breaks in hostile and country and neither do I. As an NCO I hold to the believe you look after your men and they will look after you, neither Morgan or I ever had to look back to see if our men were following, soldiers who trust their leaders will follow them into the valley of the shadow. Less than 10 minutes later Morgan waves me in, I take one final look I see nothing unusual but my gut tells me we are being watched, the day although bright and sunny I feel a darkness in me shaking it off I return to the group. The Lt. agrees with Sgt Pryce that they need to scout the Valley but we head north a spell then hope to stay parallel with the gathering hostiles, just before we saddle up I go to the packhorse and remove 2 sawed off double barrelled shotguns and shells both had custom leather slings so to hang down your back but can be brought into line real quick, in a close in brawl a couple shotguns can make the difference.

For the next part of the patrol Ahiga and I will be the forward scouts like his older brother the Navajo warrior is a tracker and warrior with few equals not much gets by him a couple miles ahead is a depression from a long dried up river and some low hills. Folks that are not familiar with the plains and prairie think it is flat like pool table but that is not the case the land is filled with small hills ravines and valleys by the rivers, a General could hide a whole army and ambush can come from anywhere. Rifles in hand we slowly approach the low ground I move right and Ahiga moves to his left I hate low ground to exposed sweat begins to break out on my forehead and palms and I ain't to proud to say I am scared clear down to my toenails. My muscles tense up waiting for the impact of an enemies bullet or arrow, damn its quiet well nothing for it I keep moving forward after what seemed hours but in reality was about 20 minutes we are both through safely and find no one, satisfied Ahiga waves the rest of the patrol forward, now that was not fun.

Once through the likely ambush spot the Lt. calls a 10 minute halt to rest the horses and have a quick smoke, Morgan says it is getting late and we as forward scouts are to look for a good place to hole up for the night, with that I am back in the saddle and moving out Ahiga and I ride north about an hour before west to my great pleasure we are seeing fewer pony tracks and that means fewer Indians. After a couple hours riding we begin to search for a good spot for a night camp, it will be a cold camp with no fire protection and good fighting ground is what is important now, we got enough water for a couple days, but I will tell you what this Little Raven is keeping me from my coffee and some son of a bitch is going to pay dearly for this sacrifice I am making.

The summer sun is beginning to set in the west when we come across a small group of low grassy mounds sitting close together with out backs to the small hills we have our flank covered and a good field of fire if attacked, it does not look we are going to find much better, before we start to set up the camp we take a quick search and find nothing out of the ordinary, we can see the rest of our group in the distance they should get here just before the sun fades in the horizon. Ahiga and I put together a makeshift picket line for the horses we are dead if we are put afoot, the plains tribes are the best horse stealers in the world. We are just about to unsaddle when the Lt. arrives with his small group before they can dismount the Navajo scout Yazie lets out a gargled yell before he falls from his horse with an Arapaho arrow through his throat. Suddenly figures appear out of the blinding setting sun and their are lot of them, without hesitation the 1st Sgt tells us to mount we are Cavalry and fight best from horse back, I look to Tse and for the first time since I have known him I see him smile but it ain't friendly, revolver in hand the Lt gives the command to charge with war whoops and rebel yells we charge, damn I love my work.

We are outnumbered at least 2 to 1 and our charge surprises our attackers they figured us to stand and fight, if I am going to be killed I want to be riding a horse when it happens, bullets arrows and spears fill the air as both lines come together soon as we got in close Morgan and I cut loose with our scatterguns 4 charges of buckshot at close range can cause fearful damage 3 Arapaho are blasted from their saddles another swaying on his horse out of the fight. Our lines meet I use my shotgun as club now swinging hard smashing a warrior and caving in the side of his skull, the scouts are fighting like demons possessed the enemy are beginning to loose a lot of warriors. We are now on the ground fighting is hand to hand sixguns, knives, tomahawks and fists, I catch a glance at the Lt. a big Cheyenne is charging him as the young officer is trying to reload his service revolver the Sgt Major taught him well he drops his six gun and pulls out the nasty looking Arkansas toothpick, I cannot help I got my own problems a big Cheyenne with a spear is trying to gut me he lunges I move aside and trip him up as soon as he hits the ground I am on him, I turn him and punch him in the face until it is a gory mess, now the madness is on me I look for another enemy to kill. The Navajo scouts are deadly fighters and love the cold steel, most using 2 long thin bladed knives in which they slash cut and stab, Tse and Ahiga are standing back to back a pile of dead Arapaho beginning to form around them both looking wild with the enemies blood covering them and their blades dripping blood. The days before the tribe killer Kit Carson and the military marched them on the Trail of Tears the Navajo were the mightiest of all the tribes not even the Apache wanted to fight them, not only warriors but grew corn and other crops and raised huge herds of sheep, their women skilled in making decorated blankets and beautiful jewellery made from silver and sea blue turquoise, Navajo blankets are few and sought after and prized by their owners.

It is hell and chaos all wrapped into one hell of a battle and the losers died, I look around for my next opponent and as my sanity returns I see there are only 3 hostiles left alive as we surround and close in on them the scouts knives thirsting for more blood, all 3 wisely drop their weapons and go to their knees singing their death songs. The 1st Sgt orders everyone to stand down and the scouts to secure the captives hands and a strong reminder that they are not to be killed, Ahiga loudly voiced his anger and frustration but tells his men to tie them up and do not be to gentle about it.

The captives now restrained the Lt. asks Tse to ask the warriors their names, using hand sign language he asks their names, 2 of the men answer with their names one is Arapaho the other a Cheyenne sub Chief named Red Hawk, the smallest and meanest looking refuses to answer reminds me of a rat, it is now pretty much full dark, I gather some small pieces of wood and some dried buffalo chips and build up a fire, I do not give a shit if it draws a thousand hostiles I will have coffee. Now at times old Morgan shows his mean side and rushes the rat faced captive, he grabs him by his shirt front and backhands him twice and Morgan has heavy fists, blood flows from the mans mouth, the Sgt pulls his wicked looking bowie knife from its sheath he pulls the bleeding mans face close to his their eyes lock in hatred and menace Morgan then tells Tse to translate." Pay attention Indian I am only going to ask one more time and if you do not answer I am going to cut your throat and cut your eyes so your spirit will wander dark and lost forever, I do not say this as a threat but a promise now asshole what is your name"? The rat face hesitates what did not know is Sgt Pryce can be real sudden, with a flick of his wrist the needle sharp tip of the bowie knife slices through the little mans right eye, Morgan now brings his knife up to take out the mans left eye, this is to much for the Arapaho he shatters in an almost inhuman scream he calls out his name.

"Little Raven".

CHAPTER 4

BACK TO THE BARN

I had not paid much attention to the goings on Morgan and I have been together a long while I know him better then my own brothers, and that Little Raven was smart to talk because Morgan don't bluff. I get the fire started and the coffee going then go over to our pack animal to retrieve the first aid kit soon my guys are going to feel the pain of their injuries, the Lt took a bullet through the meaty part of his left shoulder, painful but not to serious, both Tse and Ahiga have knife wounds, one other the remaining scouts has a broken arm and a nasty gash along his ribs, I myself have an Arapaho arrow stuck in the calf of my leg and Morgan not even a hangnail. Through time and experience I have become a pretty fair field medic, just enough knowledge to patch them up and hold them together until we can get them to the fort's hospital. Both Morgan and I were very proud of the young Lt. who refuses treatment until everyone's wounds were tended to, after doing what I can for the men it is time to get the arrow out, arrows are dirty and if left in will fester and get infected and I aim keeping both legs, thank you very much. Morgan and Tse will take the arrow out they both know what must be done unhappily I know as well I will have to dig deep it will not do to show weakness especially with the Navajo scouts to who courage and strength is praised above all other things. My stomach turns over as 2 big knife blades are stuck deep in the glowing coals to heat, ok Laddie iron on iron hard today remember who you are Ahiga hands me a thick leather strip to bite on so I don't break my teeth.

The Lt is kneeling at my feet and has my injured leg secured so not to move around to much, first thing Morgan has to do is cut off the feather end of the arrow this is where the fun starts, using a smaller knife he begins to run the sharp blade around the shaft slowly cutting deeper into the wood when the knife gets close to through he breaks off the feathered end. Red pain explodes through my body I bite hard and sweat cause but damn was the easy part. Tse now grabs the arrow just behind the flint tip and gets ready to pull it through I nod for him to go ahead without warning he pulls the bloody wooden shaft through blood pours from the wound, "DAMN", that hurt, my medics make sure both the entrance and exit wounds were bleeding freely to get the bad blood out, I do not dare look but I know that the red hot knives are out of the fire as the knives sear the wounds shut I growl and curse through the leather strap, man I never want to do this again, I can still smell my burning flesh.

It is done I am done and know I am going to pass out, before I go black I tell Morgan have someone wake me I will take the last watch, I remember nothing after that until Morgan gives me a shake and asks if I am ok to do guard duty he will pull it if I want,. I decline of course it would shame me to no end shirking my duties over a little leg wound, but I did have to ask my Pard to help me up and hand me my shotgun, morning will be here soon and thankfully we will be back in the saddle. I hobble over to where Ahiga is watching the prisoners, they are all sleeping or pretending to be I sit gingerly and put the shotgun beside me for a quick grab if it is needed, Ahiga says nothing but pats me on the shoulder as he heads back to his bed. The eastern sky is beginning to show some colour now the meadowlarks and other morning birds are beginning to greet the day, I have always love this time of the day a few moments and calm before the rigors of the day, to my great delight Morgan brings me a hot mug of coffee and a cigar, he sits and we talk quiet for a few minutes mostly on how well the young Lt handled himself in his first battle, the Sgt Major would be popping his brass buttons with pride. The Lt is thinking we should send one of the scouts as a courier take an extra horse and ride hell for leather to get word to the fort Commander the 1st Sgt readily agrees and as the Lt. writes Tse gets one of his scouts to catch up a good mount and do not stop riding until he gets back to the fort.

The next 2 days riding back are brutal most of us fighting pain and have dangerous prisoners to watch I look forward and I am near tears as I see the fort in the distant summer haze we continue to ride until we are about a half mile from the fort when the 1st Sgt calls a halt saying we will do our best to look sharp riding into the fort heads high tall and straight in the saddle, I do the best with what I have, the Lt. then leads off with Morgan and myself behind him then the scouts with our prisoners. The Commander has called the whole Regiment out on parade to receive us back, my leg is forgotten I sit straight eyes forward this is why you wear the uniform and take pride in belonging to something important and bigger than yourself not only for you but those who came before you and those who will serve and die after you, once a soldier always a soldier.

With their leader captured and shamed the warriors knew their medicine is bad and broke off in small groups back to their reservations, so no messiah now more Indian war not bad for shave tail Lt, 2 old war horse Sgts and some damn fine scouts.

Long live the Black Knights.

PRIDE IS A PERSONAL COMMITMENT. IT IS AN ATTITUDE WHICH SEPERATES EXCELLANCE FROM MEDIOC

STORY 3

RIDING FOR THE BRAND

CHAPTER 1

WHERE THE LEATHER IS SCARRED, THERE IS A STORY TO TELL

I try to ignore my shame riding an old plug of a horse, flat busted and have not eaten in 2 days I was told the Double M were looking for trail hands to take a herd to Kansas, I hear the snickers I keep my head high and straight ahead until I come upon a group of men having coffee around a campfire. I do not dismount and wait to be invited to coffee the smell food cooking makes my head swims but I try not to show my distress. There are 3 men by the fire a big Mexican with a smile and a couple knife scars on his face, a average sized man but the reddest hair and beard I ever did see both beard and hair in need of a trim, the last man is dressed a bit better but still in range clothes his expression a blank blackboard his hair short with a touch of grey on the sides, slim but no more than 5 foot 10 I feel his pale blue eyes on me even a dumbass like me knows who the top dog is here and the man I need to talk to.

"Howdy fellas my name is Jim Thorton from the Big Sandy country fellas in town said you might be hiring for a drive up to Kansas, I am a good hand and no shirker and could surely do need the look but be obliged job or no job be obliged for a cup of coffee." The Red haired man does the talking, "They call me Triple Creek Johnson I ain't the boss but I can invite you to climb down off that crowbait and help yourself to coffee, this big mean looking hombre here is Salvador Desoto and this here is the Trail Boss and the man who does the hiring Smoke Kellerman, now lad come sit take a load off." Out of the corner of my eye I catch the Boss nodding to an older man by the chuckwagon I dismount and am handed a mug I approach the small group of men, hoping my hands don't shake I pour myself a steaming cup of black Texas crude. The Trail Boss has still said nothing I begin to feel a bit uncomfortable under his gaze I can tell he is thinking me over. Damn this maybe the best coffee I ever had been days since I had a real cup, a older man comes from the chuckwagon with a heaping plate of beans and biscuits, "Here lad get this into you hired on or not no man leaves my fire with out a meal in his guts if you want more you just holler now." After he hands me the plate of beans and fork I see him and Smoke exchange glances Cookie smiles and whistles while he heads back to the chuckwagon, I know the men I am with are real Hombres tough hard and have been tested and survived, I am so hungry I want to shovel the food down but I will not show my weakness with these men, I slowly clean my plate clean and get every biscuit crumb inside me I am feeling better already, I help myself to a second cup of the trail brew. Salvador hands me a thin black cigar I pull a sulphur from my ragged vest pocket and fire it up and inhale the strong smoke, as my eyes water and I nearly cough a lung up I hear the men chuckle.

"Well much obliged for the grub and coffee got yourselves a damn fine trail cook," I am interrupted by the Boss his voice quiet but with strength and authority, "Mr. Cooper seems a good thing because Mr. Sam our cook needs a helper and if you work out we will see about you riding herd, pay is 120 dollars and paid after delivery to the railhead in Dodge City. If you want to pull your freight before we get to Dodge you will get a horse with 2 days food and will be shot on sight if you try to return, a man should never start anything unless he plans to see it to the end." Well Jim lad the offer is on the table what do you say", "Sir that is the best offer I heard all day, my Pa taught me if you give a man your word it is a bond and a trust not to be broken, I will be with you at Dodge City, I stand and walk to the Trail Boss and extend my hand we shake his grip firm I can feel the power in him, "Ok cowboy welcome to the Double M now get your lazy ass over to the chuckwagon and see what Mr Sam needs doing, and when he talks be smart if you keep your mouth shut and your ears open that man has crossed more rivers than any of us, now scoot." Smiling I lead my horse to the chuckwagon I know it is a lucky day and this is a good outfit, Mr Sam is waiting for me I get the impression he knew all along that the boss was going to take me on, I do believe he is a sly old fox, "Thank you for the grub Sir that was first rate chow, boys are lucky to have you I hear good trail cooks are rare, The Boss told me to see you to put me to work, oh my name is Jim, Howdy."

"Well first off Jim we will drop the sir shit call me Mr. Sam, now take your gear and put it in the wagon and turn that plug loose we got plenty of good horses we will get you one later, after you are done that gather up as much firewood and dry buffalo chips for the fire then we will get supper going ok get er done Jim lad." I remove what little gear I have off my old horse it did not take long Pa's old saddle and Sharps.50 buffalo gun a worn jacket and bedroll about all I own in the world, I sure wish I could find me a revolver, trees are scarce in this part of Texas and firewood is hard to find but dried buffalo chips burn real well hot, clean and nearly smokeless. Today is a very good day for today I now ride for Smoke Kellerman and the Double M brand.

CHAPTER 2

RODE HARD AND PUT AWAY WET

The rest of the day was pretty much a blur of activity mostly I fetched and tried to stay out of the way, the men are now coming in from the range for their supper and night coffee, I get few howdy's but like most outfits you have to earn their respect and prove you can saddle your own broncs. It as it should be but there is one other young cowboy about my age named Billy Gibbons friendly and wild as the Texas wind, I recon never gets boring around Billy. Now I will tell you what any person who thinks a trail cooks life is easy is a dumbass the day starts during middle of night making sure the fire is kept up and there is coffee for the nights herders, breakfast has to be started and ready for the hands before first light, then the tin cups and plates have to washed and put away, then we have to hook up the team to the chuckwagon and break camp then on the move to set up for the noon meal, i have no idea how Mr. Sam has managed all these years but he has it down to an artform.

Mr. Sam being a wise man uses big mules to pull the wagon, a matching pair of blue roan draft Jennies, Penelope and Phoebe named after some old world goddesses, people tend to look down on mules, but mules are tougher stronger smarter and many times faster than horses, and when going through Indian country there is less threat them being stolen seems Indians ain't fond of mule meat. I am driving the team they are a dream to handle with a few cuss words from Mr. Sam, Pa always told me if you want to learn watch and ask questions, sound advise. I ask Mr. Sam, "The boss Smoke I keep thinking I should know the name but just cannot figure out why, he ain't overly big but he walks real tall, the men seem to like him." Cookie laughs and gives me friendly pat on the shoulder, "Well Jim you got a good eye for judging men because Smoke Kellerman is probably the most dangerous man in any mans territory, he is streak lighting with his hog legs and hits what he aims at I seen his graveyards, he will fight you anyway you want knives knuckle and skull he is a wild man in a scrap the Vikings of old would have called him a Beserker. "I remember one time 4 Apache braves thought they would have some fun and came at him with knives, well lets just say he is here and they ain't, but a man who lives by the code and his word is his bond, he is a fair man and treats you right if you do your job and keep out of trouble but bad Hombre to have as an enemy. "Mercer and Mason sent for him personal cause they know he rides for the brand and gets the job done. "Now them other men you met yesterday you watch and learn from Salvador Desoto he ramrods the horse remuda uses mostly Mexican Vaqueros they know horses better than cows used to ride the owl hoot trail until he met up with Smoke who somehow convinced him honest work was better than sleeping in caves, his boys are a tough bunch you do not ride for a man like Desoto unless you are fighter. "Now that red headed galoot is Triple Creek Johnson, he is Smoke's right hand straw boss but the men know when he talks he speaks for the boss, his real name is Ben but he got into a gun fight in Triple Creek Arizona with 3 bad men they were treated to a first rate funeral on boot hill, I never seen a better man with a Winchester rifle and a knows cattle,

Jim lad would you by chance be kin to Donald Thorton came from Arkansas moved down west Texas way?"

I damn near fall off the wagon seat shocked by the question I knew Pa did some cowboying in his hell for leather days but he never talked much about it, "My Pa's name was Donald most folks called in Don, both he and Ma came from Pine Bluff in Arkansas, Pa never spoke much of his early days I always got the feeling something bad happened but Pa up and died before I could find out why, did you really know my Pa?" Mr. Sam tells me Smoke, Pa and himself rode together and raised all sorts of hell damn fine cowman and saddle Pard, I don't think he would mind me telling you now. We were down to Fort Worth doing some drinking and a little gambling between riding jobs when your Pa was set upon and challenged by a would be gunslinger named Kid Bravo, your Pa had no choice but to talk with his guns, when the hot lead stopped and the smoke cleared the Kid was shot to doll rags but he got off a couple wild shots one that killed a young woman and mother walking on the street. "Don blamed himself for the woman's death no matter how Smoke and I tried to tell the stubborn knot head it was not his fault just bad luck he just got quiet and sullen then one morning we woke and he had ridden out and we ain't seen him since, Jim your old man was one of the good ones and Smoke will back me up on it, well I will be damned Don Cooper's son." Well time to make noon camp I sure wish Pa would of spoke to me of I would have understood, he always was stubborn as jackass, hope it is a good place to find wood.

I am excited the last minute jobs were getting done everything was hurried everyone having much to do with little time to do it Smoke put out the word the herd was heading to Kansas tomorrow morning, it was a quick noon camp, beef sandwiches and coffee. Before I know it we are moving again to set up our last camp before we hit the trail, I sure hope the boss lets me ride herd some. Although just past 16 I know wherever you go there are assholes and bullies, I am doing the supper dishes when a couple dirty greasy looking men both beady eyed rat faces, Chet Bundy the bigger of the two is in front throws his plate and cup in the wash bucket intentionally hard as to cover me with soapy water the 2nd man Chet's cousin Elmer copies his cousin and slashes me with soapy water, Chet gives off a mean sounding laugh and calls out to Mr. Sam, "Cookie looks like your boy here went and got hisself all wet, I recon its tough getting good cooks helpers these days, sure is a pretty helper." Both men laugh, well that tears it I wipe the soap from my face and remove my long white apron, "Ok you big son a bitch you want some of me come get it or are you all mouth." Fingers that feel like steel claws dig into my shoulder and I find it is Smoke holding unto my shoulder he has a hard look about him I then notice Mr. Sam come from the wagon with a sawed off double barreled 12 gauge holding it barrel down by his side, releasing his grip on my shoulder he speaks to the rat faces, "You 2 men drop your six guns and put them aside, ok Jim which one to you want first, it will be fair fight with no interference unless you are loco enough to face Mr. Sam's greener, now Jim which one do you want?" "Boss I want that big asshole I am going to tear his wheelhouse down." The other riders form a circle where the around the big rat face and myself, spitting I put my dukes up and advance on the big man, only the speed of youth saves me as the brute unleashes a wild left hook that would have taken my head clear off, but I managed to turn enough for it to be glancing blow even at that I felt his power and I now know I am in big trouble. I figure my best weapon is speed hit fast and move back quick, well that plan did not last long I take a hard shot to the ribs then thrown heavily to the ground, the big man grinning now gets close to put the boots to me, the loud click of a shotgun hammer stops him. I manage to struggle up rat face is to eager for the kill and leaves himself open I let go a straight right hand from the shoulder and feel the satisfaction of feeling his nose break and watch the blood flow. The big man is stunned for a second then he lets out a great roar and then proceeds to beat the hell out of me, I go deep into the darkness.

CHAPTER 3

BLUE HAWK

A hand shaking my shoulder wakes me, it is light damn I slept in, Cookie hands me a cup of hot coffee, I apologize more than once feeling shamed of letting Mr. Sam down, "Jim Lad you get that coffee in you we are moving out soon, and no worries I somehow muddled through without you and you took a hell of a beating boy but that Shit head Chet Bundy looks like a ring tailed racoon with a nose that looks like a smashed tomato, you watch out for them the smaller one is Elmer Bundy he has the look of a back shooter to me, now drink up and lets get er going lad." I fail horribly on my first attempt to get to my feet, I stifle a scream as the pain smashes through me, more slowly I rise finally on my feet I get a bit dizzy but goes away quick digging deep I take my first painful step of what I expect to be a very long day. Damn I hate being right but my to my surprise throughout the day Smoke, Salvador, Triple Creek, Billy and a few of the boys came by to see how I was making out and hazed me a might with some good natured kidding, makes me feel good like I am part of something and pride riding with tall men.

After 3 days on the trail the cattle fall into a rhythm we are lucky we have a good lead steer a big brown and white longhorn steer named Moses, now a good lead cow is worth 5 cowboys Moses as on other drives moves to the front and will be there every day on the drive the herd follows where he goes, Moses is not for sale and will be taken back to the home range. My bruises are turning a nice shade of yellow and purple but even though I got wiped good Chet Bundy's smashed nose is a nasty mess and the circles around his eyes are still visible, gives me a certain sense of pleasure watching his discomfort. Keeping your eyes open and your mouth shut is wise advice I start to notice things like none of the riders carry rifles when working cattle to cumbersome and wear the gun belts high so not to get snagged. Late afternoon Triple Creek comes along side the chuckwagon," a very good afternoon Mr. Sam I would like to take Jim lad off your hands for a spell I spotted a herd of big mule deer aways back some venison might make a nice change in the pot, I will need some help bringing them back and Jim here needs to learn the country a bit." In mock anger Mr. Sam tells Triple Creek that I should be doing something other than loafing on the wagon seat but he is to have me back for supper cleanup, it is all a game with cowboys no matter how old they tend to be boys, Triple Creek already had a nice looking Bay gelding saddled and ready I go to the back of the wagon and fetch my big.50 buffalo gun and shells.

Triple Creek whistles when he sees the big gun," Damn Jim that cannon should have wheels on it, gun like that could break a mans shoulder if handled wrong, well let's get going we will see how good you are with the Sharps, damn effective weapon in the right hands, well grab a hunk of mane and lets get moving before Cookie gets the vapors." The ride away was a mixture of laughter and cussing, sure feels good to be on a horse again and the bay is a fine animal smooth gait, good speed and smart someone who knew what they were doing trained this horse. We are headed towards a small ravine and creek about a mile east of the herd from this direction we will come up wind of deer feeding giving us a good chance for a shot. Dismounting short of the ravine edge and with rifles if front across our arms we crawl real slow to the edge removing our sombrero's before looking down into the small valley, not more than 60 yards away there is a big buck and 4 does all a good size, there is no way to get closer so we will have to shoot from here using sign he tells me he will take the buck and if a chance the female to the right, I am to pick the far left doe with luck we might get 3 but we want the big buck lots of meat on him. I wait for Triple Creek to fire I snug the butt of the rifle into my shoulder and lay my sights just behind the front shoulder the best chance for a clean kill, I have a spare cartridge out for a second shot, Triple Creek fires my shot a split second later the buck and doe are down I eject the spent cartridge and slam in the second big shell and cock the hammer back, the doe is now close to 90 yards away and moving fast, I take a breath and hold it then leading the running deer I fire my second shot and give off a whoop, damn fine shot if I do say so myself, I knew before I looked that my shooting partner brought down his 2 deer looks like it will be venison stew and steaks for a spell.

"That was one hell of a shot Jim lad your Pa was a master gunman with any weapon especially the long gun he taught me shooting, you learned your lessons well he would be proud now go grab your horse and bring haul it back we will just gut them before hauling them back to camp." Behind me I hear a branch snap I quickly spin my rifle around and find an very old Indian standing no more than 10 feet from us, Triple Creek is holding his rifle in a pistol grip with hammer back, trust nothing in the wilderness, the old man looks frail and starving looking past him I can see some women and kids all having that hollow stare of hunger and fear.

Pointing my Sharps at the ground I carefully put the hammer back down showing the old man I do not aim to harm him, Triple Creek moves his sights off the old man and lowers his Winchester, the man is old his hair long thin and silver, his buckskins and moccasins are beautifully made but now looking thin and worn like the old Indian he approaches slowly his arms held open to show he has no hidden weapon there is no fear in his eyes. Death would be easy and he probably prays for it but he still has some of his people to care for before he crosses over. The old man has tattoos around his eyes which is common with the Caddo's and Witchita's I grew up around Caddo's and can speak some and understand some if not spoken to fast both Tribes use a common language speaking in Caddo I speak to the old man. "Welcome Grandfather it appears you have trouble I am named Jim Thorton and this is my friend Triple Creek, Grandfather who are you and why are you away from your tribe." The old mans face shows surprise when he hears me speak in Caddo, the old man takes a moment as to prepare his words before speaking, with a voice still strong and full of power responds, "I am Blue Hawk of the Witchita's once I held power and was respected as a good leader but when to many summers pass the hair turns to snow your voice is no longer heard in the fire circle, Small Horse now leads our people and has more love for white mans crazy water than in his people, many of the warriors will trade anything for a bottle, the village has gone crazy." "I fear for the safety of the women and children so I take them away but we have no weapons to hunt and food is scarce we heard the shots and hoped to find food, I am an old man and do not eat much but my people starve, I am still an old wolf and will not beg but I ask you to share your meat with my people."

I look to Triple Creek with a nod of agreement we move to the horses and remove 2 of the does and place them on the ground, Blue Hawk calls for the women to come and start skinning the animals, there were 11 people with Blue Hawk a mixture of women, kids and young men a couple years short of becoming warriors. Triple Creek and I meet with Blue Hawk, my Pard hands the old man a myself a cigar I see Blue Hawks eyes smile just a bit by the unexpected treat, we talk and smoke a bit I watch amazed how skillfully and quickly the Witchita women skin and clean the animals, it is time we are heading back before we go Blue hawk has an older woman bring him a leather necklace and pouch Blue Hawk asks me to remove my big hat and places the necklace around my neck, "Strong Medicine for there are many dangers awaiting you, your name will be spoke around the camp fires as a man who fights like a wolf, this I have seen in my visions, farewell friends."

Turns out old Triple Creek is a gabber and enjoys the role of story teller and wastes no time flapping his gums about our hunting trip I have to admit I did secretly enjoy hearing tell of the nice shot I made to bring down the fast moving deer. Smoke stands and listens to his old friends tale a small smile creeps into his hard eyes, Triple Creek is a man who can spin a yarn in which everything gets bigger in the next telling, Smoke motions to me to join him we take a short walk just out of hearing distance of the camp. "Jim lad you are coming along real well you are earning the respect of most of the men myself included and you know well enough that Indians respect courage above all, a cowboy it is all about respect. As with anything worthwhile you got to earn, also like to thank you in the way you treated Blue Hawk we know each other your Pa knew him as well, when we were all young lions Blue Hawk was one a hell of a warrior. "After we got done trying to kill each other respect replaced killing and we have been blood brothers for years, a fine man still looking after his people the best you can, now that's what I call riding for the brand hope he and his people make out alright," reaching under his shirt Smoke pulls out from under his shirt a leather necklace and bag almost the same as mine telling me Blue Hawk gave him his many years ago and seeing he is still above the flowers he believes in its magic. "Jim tomorrow you become a cowboy Shorty got himself banged when his horse hit a gopher hole so he can help Mr. Sam and you will be working the drive you are going to work with Billy he is young but that boy knows cows, now come with me a minute I have something for you."

We head to the chuckwagon Smoke pulls his war bag out of the back and rummages through it until he finds and pulls out a six gun in a well made brown leather belt and holster and hands it to me," you will need a sidearm in case of trouble this is a fine weapon a .45 Smith and Wesson Schofield one of the best hog legs made, accurate and hits hard take care of it and it will take care of you. Remember now when you are working cow critters to keep it high on your waist so not to get tangled, now get some rest you will damn well need it." Laughing to himself the Boss walks back to the campfire, I walk to my blankets and crawl in before I go to sleep I check out the Schofield all chambers were filled as well as the bullet loops on the back of the well tooled gun belt, Damn what a day.

CHAPTER 4

HARD LESSONS

Morning darkness finds me and Billy warming up with cookies horseshoe floating black coffee, inside I am excited and jumpy but hopefully not showing it much, I see Salvador and approach him, "Hefe would any of your Vaqueros have a spare Leather Lariat I ain't much with a rope, well got to run Billy is getting fidgety, obliged to you Salvador." Senor Desoto tells me as I am walking to my horse he will ask around and he hopes I enjoy my first day riding drag I hear his laughs as we ride away towards the herd. I recon riding drag on a herd is about a cowboys least favorite job you ride behind the herd to make sure the cattle keep moving and watch for any strays in dry country like we are in now we have to wear bandanas over our noses and mouth the dust so thick can hardly see the last cows ass at 6 feet, and just to add to the fun the horse and deer flies attack unmercifully, but today I do not care I am in the hurricane deck and not a wagon seat.

Billy slows down his horse and we get a bit of distance away from the dust, as usual Smoke is right Billy is a natural born cowboy and is a wealth of knowledge I become a sponge listening and asking questions, thankfully Billy is a first class riding partner and he is patient with a knothead like myself. About an hour later I see one of the Vaqueros riding hell for leather towards us, damn them boys can ride, he pulls his horse to a skidding stop, then with a big grin hands me a beautifully made leather lariat, "Amigo the boss Salvador sends me to give you this lariat and he says to tell you that if you loose it or damage it he will make a new one from your hide, "waving dust from his face he says he has to get back to the horses slapping his big horse on the rear with his big sombrero and a giving off a yell he is off like a shot from a cannon. Billy checks out the braided leather rope and nods his approval leather is more flexible with a bit of give most southern Texas riders prefer the leather lariat when working cattle.

Pa always said be careful what you wish for after the first grueling week I feel like I have been worked like a rented mule, long time in the saddle go through 3 or 4 horses a day, meals were inhaled with coffee then there is night herding grab a few hours and up long before the sun it is a grind and vicious circle of routine until we come to our first big river crossing then fear and chaos rule. I will admit I am more than a little nervous being my first go at it, Billy tells me to use the buckskin horse good swimmer and has made rivers crossing before and if I get into trouble give the buckskin its head and trust him to get you out, then he tells me Smoke says if I drown he is going to be very displeased being down a rider. We both give off a laugh but know Smoke truly cares for and frets for the safety of his riders and the men know it this is a bond which makes the Double M riders a hard, tight group best to be left alone, I stroke the buckskins neck and speak quiet to him I can feel his heartbeat it is quick like mine with an eagerness and excitement this is one hell of a horse and likes it tough, I take a deep breath and approach the rivers edge.

Billy and me are downstream of the herd doing our best to keep the swimming and drifting cattle together and pushing them to the far side, what a wild ride, yells, curses horses and men screaming the loud mooing of the herd we are well over half way across when something underwater and unseen spooks Billy's horse putting the young cowboy is the river and he is in trouble as the drifting cattle close in on him and then with nowhere to go will drown. Well to hell with that I move the buckskin as close as can to my Pard and with a prayer I toss the lariat I feel a sense of relief as I see Billy's hand snatch it up and I feel his weight on the leather, I do not try to pull him in but point the buckskin to shore digging in my spurs for speed that damn horse got us out and safely to land I dismount and pull my half drowned friend out of the water. I look back at the river and get a shiver at how fast things can go to hell and me with in it, takes most of the day to get the herd across and gathered up, but the river would have its payment Miles Rogers a tall easy going rider did not survive the crossing, he and his horse went under his horse came up but poor Miles never did. We searched for him but the river was keeping its prize, with no body to bury Smoke gathered the men and said a few words, then we are back in the hurricane deck heading north once more.

Next morning my cloths are dry and I am happy that damn river is behind me, I try not to think of the next one, man that was one wild ride, Smoke rides up and joins me, taking out a couple of the thin black Mexican cigars and hands me one, after firing up the strong smoke he tells me. "Mr. Thorton that was a good piece of work you did yesterday Billy told me the fix you got out him out of and how you risked your life for him, Jim your Pa would be real proud, we just make you into a top hand yet, now get your ass back to work we got miles to make, see you for supper." As he always does when he finishes what he has to say he is off to address the unending tasks he has as trail boss and I thank my lucky stars my first trail drive is with him and the other boys, Billy is well liked and the crew are happy we survived well all except the Bundy polecats, those boys seem to run on pure mean and hate. It is a good day on the trail we are getting into some short grass so the dust is down, a warm day with a sweet cool breeze Billy and I talked and hazed strays back into the herd the day passes quickly and we do make some miles it has become my custom to sit and chew the fat with Mr. Sam after supper, the man is full of knowledge and a good talker and he treated me real good when I joined the outfit. Billy and I have night herd in less than 3 hours so I head to my blankets just as I am settling in I hear a strange soft voice coming from the darkness calling out Jim Thorton I need speak to Jim Thorton or Triple Creek, Blue Hawk sends me to tell you big trouble big trouble coming.

Smoke and Triple Creek walk up and join me, Smoke orders the men to keep their hands off their weapons I call to the voice in the dark that it is safe to enter the camp no one will harm him, seconds later I see a young teen appear as if by magic out of the darkness. I invite him to the fire and offer him coffee and sugar, once settled around the fire the young warrior tells us his name is Crow and his chief Blue Hawk has sent him to tell us that Lone Wolf and at least 50 Kiowa warriors are waiting to ambush you for your horses guns and food, "we do not know exactly where he will attack you but soon you get into the Snake Back hills the low hills make it a good place to kill you Blue Hawk prays to the great spirit that you survive, now I must get back they need me." From the chuckwagon we hear, "hold on a minute Crow before you go take this with you we got extra, "Mr. Sam hands the youth a large burlap bag filled with sugar, flower, coffee, canned fruit and jerky, Smoke hands Crow a couple cigars and tells him to thank his great friend and bother Blue Hawk he will be remembered for his bravery and good spirit, the young man sling the burlap bag over his shoulder and without a word vanishes back into the night.

Well looks like there will be no sleep tonight ain't much use trying to sleep Billy and I have another coffee and smoke before riding out for our shift to keep the cattle company, most cowboys like to sing in low voices as they ride seems to calm the animals, now Billy has a pleasant to the ear voice I could not carry a tune in a bucket, so I hum song I remember Ma singing, I sure miss Ma. The men back in camp will be making war talk trying to figure how to get the herd past the Kiowa's and more importantly staying alive doing it but if that old scoundrel Lone Wolf thinks we are easy pickings he has made a big mistake. Salvador has 8 battle hardened Vaqueros who have fought and survived the Apache for centuries, Smoke and Triple Creek 2 of the most deadly men anywhere in the west and 14 iron on iron tough trail hardened cowboys who do not think much of the Kiowas plans. There is one thing the Indians never figured out and that is cattle or have any understanding of the thundering power of a herd on the run like a wall falling on you, a tough way to go under hundreds of hard hooves I hope this is something we can use to our advantage, but above my head let the big boys sort it out one thing I know sure is then Kiowas are tough and damn fine fighters, this could get real bloody.

CHAPTER 5

BATTLE ON THE SNAKES BACK

A couple saddle weary cowboys ride back to the campfire in the grey of the pr- dawn light I feel the test of my strength and will is just beginning, hope I got the sand for it. My concern is not so much my safety but a fear of letting the good men I ride with down, I notice as we ride in men have attached their rifle scabbards to their saddles fully loaded rifles in the boots, from now on we all ride loaded for bear.

The Kiowa war chief Lone Wolf sits alone staring into the small fire his thoughts on the future and his status among his tribe once he kills the men who move cattle he will have fine weapons, many good horses and much food he will be the one true and only leader of the Kiowa nation no one will dare challenge his claim rule. He will then bring all the warriors together and wipe out every white man, woman and child in northern Texas. Lone wolf looks at his round shield, the black head of a wolf was painted on the face of the shield, from the bottom of the shield are 2 long wolf tales, the great medicine man Mamanti (he who walks above) has prayed over the shield and has put powerful magic into the strong hide, Mamanti has told him as long as he holds the shield no bullets can harm him and the great spirit watches over and protects him, the time for war is now.

The war council is still going on when we get back to the campfire and life giving coffee, Smoke is pumping Joe Murphy one of the older hands and knew this part of the country, the last couple days of travel the herd has had little water or grazing, a mournful mooing for water goes through herd. "Joe once through the Snakes back how far is it to water these critters will be desperate for water soon and I am hoping to use that to our advantage ain't no force on earth that can stop a herd of dry mouthed cattle who get the scent of water, so Joe tell me something good Pard." The old cowboy smiles a big grin minus a few teeth he is enjoying being the centre of attention, "Well boss about 2 miles past the Snakes Back there is Shinbone Creek not wide but nice and deep enough for the herd good water I seen cows smell water over 5 miles away by the time we reach the Snake they are to be moving quick we may lose a few but the pesky Kiowa's are in for a big surprise if they try to stop them." Smoke nods his approval and thanks Joe then tells him to hit the blankets going to be a hell of a few days coming up he takes one of his strong black cigars bites off the tip and then fires it up with a sulphur before giving us our orders, "Men looks like old Lone Wolf is looking for a scrap I recon we the Double M riders will give him all he can hold and then some no damn Kiowa is stopping this drive or taking this herd, we are going to Dodge city so here is what I figure we do and if any of you hear something that don't sound right speak up, now to the rat killing."

"Salvador my Amigo I want you to mix the horse herd in with the cattle before we make our run over the Snakes back and I will need 2 of your Vaqueros to stay with the herd, Triple Creek you, Billy, Jim and the 2 of Salvador's men are going to stay and push the herd and I do mean push and push hard we need thins to happen quick. Now boys you are going to be in the hot seat and exposed but once you start you cannot stop for anything if any Kiowa's get in your way shoot them or run over them but do not stop, to stop is almost certain death by either arrows or hooves. "Mr. Jim I am putting Joe and Rex in the wagon with Winchesters stay as close to the herd as possible but like I told the other boys no stopping I hope them mules are as good as you say, now the rest of us are going to be Cavalry riding hard and fast to smash into their main force and provide covering fire for the men and herd. "Fella's I don't cotton to saying this but when the battle starts and all sorts of hell breaks loose we will all have to take a cowboys chance if a man goes down he will have to fend for himself until we can get help to him, you men know what's expected of you I know every man will do his best. I recon someone should have warned that Kiowa villain that the Double M is one tough and salty outfit and those that interfere with our affairs wish they hadn't. "There is an old fable of a man chasing a tiger seems he was doing fine until he caught it then the game changed, now think things over and we will look at it fresh in the morning which seems about 2 hours away. We will not make many miles today I want to hold the cattle short of Snakes Back and the smell of the water I want them beeves thirsty now break it up and get some rack time."

Billy the mad cap looks to me smiling my Amigo lives for the thrill of action and danger this ride is right in his wheelhouse I cannot help but smile back, my youth ignorance and the feeling of invincibility makes my blood flow hot and eager for action, damn the young are dumbasses. The Buckskin and I wait in the morning pre dawn grey waiting now to make our run through and over the Snake Back, I am not feeling near as brave this morning my heartbeat is faster, my mouth dry, palms wet, cursing quietly I dry them on my shirt and take a couple deep breaths then check the Schofield for about the 10th time. I can just see Billy's outline ahead of me thankfully it will be soon now I am much better doing than waiting, time to get er done. Smoke gives the signal we start moving the herd slow and quiet, our lead steer is a big Texas longhorn lead steer and gets real riled when someone or something blocks his way we wait to see how he gets along with them Kiowa's.

The massive steer moves up taking his place at the head of the herd and gets the herd in a walk Billy and I are on the left side of the herd Triple Creek and a young Vaquero named Sanchez are on the right and another Vaquero bringing up the rear Mr. Sam and his wagon are behind me and just back of the herd. The horse herd is brought up by Salvador and his men and merged in with the cattle then join Smoke and the other mounted men rifles out and ready for war. The cows are getting real thirsty the mooing mournful almost pleading suddenly the massive head of the lead steer head comes up he comes to a stop a raises his nose smelling the air I can tell he can smell water, he starts off again but this time his pace is faster and more determined by now the whole herd has smelled water looking forward I can now see the hills of the Snake Back looks like I will say it is a great place for an ambush.

Smoke gives Triple Creek the signal to let it rip with a rebel war cry Triple Creek snaps a cow on the ass with his rope we pull our big hats down tight and dig in our spurs the buckskin responds immediately bolting out deer fast. The big animal in front knows the noises of upcoming trouble and that tough old mossy horn loves a good scrap, he lets off a mighty bellow as a challenge to anyone who wants some and then begins the run through the deadly gauntlet. I now have the .45 Schofield in my hand I can see rifle smoke and hear firing coming from the hills as we get closer we can see the Kiowa's made a crude attempt to barricade the narrow exit, an arrow slices open a deep cut just under my eye I look and see a young warrior getting ready for another shot I cut loose with my.45 the warrior screams as the jagged hot lead rips open his stomach in horror I see his guts spilling out. We are almost through I look back happy to see Mr. Sam's chuckwagon is staying up close I look over to see how Triple Creek is doing I wish I hadn't, just as I spotted him 2 arrows hit him almost at the same time, one in his upper chest and the other going trough his throat then everything goes into slow motion as I watch him slowly fall from his saddle under the hard hooves of the running cattle, damn it to hell. The huge horned beast sees the barricade he puts his head down then hits full on the flimsy structure it does does not even slow him down just then an Indian steps out his intent to kill the big steer the young Vaquero on the other side puts him under before he can get off a shot, then suddenly we are through we now leave the cattle they will not move from the water and head back to join the fray.

Throughout history in battles it seems that through fate, destiny or just the gods playing for their pleasure somehow it always has the 2 champions of their armies meeting in a life and death struggle and this battle is no different. Just as I get back within sight of the battle I see Lone Wolf slam his horse into Smoke's big gelding both men and horses go down, Smoke looses his .45 in the fall but comes up quick with a nasty looking Green River knife must be 12 inches of heavy finely honed steel, almost looks like a butchers knife, Lone Wolf is now on his feet a large bowie knife in his hand the men lock eyes and begin to circle each looking for an opening. I watch the 2 warriors in their deadly dance, both men are extremely quick and smart knife fighters, I watch fixated it reminds me of a time I watched an eagle and a rattle snake fight, quick movements strike quick get out that day the snake won and escaped but not today the snake has just made a mortal mistake. Lone Wolf feints with his shoulder hoping to lure Smoke in but he is not fighting any ordinary man, Smoke makes his own feint and the Kiowa bites overextending himself, with a mighty swipe Smoke opens his enemies throat hot blood shoots from the mans gaping wound covering Smoke with the hold sticky liquid, Smoke does not hesitate as Lone Wolf falls he grabs him by the hair and with a quick swipe of his knife takes his enemies scalp holding the scalp high in the air Smoke gives off a mighty Comanche war cry, everything stops.

The Kiowa's have had enough they look at the blood covered man holding their leaders scalp, Smoke lets out another screeching war cry, the remaining warriors become scared and nervous looking at Smoke as he were some sort of evil spirit, then as if by some unseen signal they begin to run or ride away and are not looking back, in disgust Smoke throws the bloody skin and hair to the ground. The battle of Snake Back is over and we still got a herd, we won but we paid a high price Triple Creek, Joe and the Vaquero riding drag did not live to finish the ride, we find what's left of our friend Triple

Creek he is so battered and torn I turn my head for fear of puking I sure hope them arrows killed him first, "Damn". Joe just had pure bad luck as he was about to take a shot the wagon hit a rock and knocked him off the wagon seat unto the ground when we find him he has at least 12 arrows in him but in front of him are 3 dead Kiowa warriors Joe went out hard like the wolf. The young Vaquero just had a lone arrow in the middle of his back but it went in deep ripping lungs and heart, at least he died quick, death is much better than the brutality of the Kiowa, especially the women. Many of the men have wounds but nothing to serious we were extremely lucky in that, my cheek stings putting my fingers to it I remember the arrow cut my fingers are covered in blood from the still bleeding cut I surely do hope someone is a good hand with a needle and thread, damn this should be fun. We gather up our dead and will re group at the creek, Smoke leaves a couple men to destroy any of the enemies weapons, I will tell you what that was one hell of a ride and I am not ashamed to say I am right pleased I survived.

CHAPTER 6

KANSAS RAIDERS

Why am I not surprised when it is Mr. Sam sewing up my cheek that man seems to always taking care of me, he is a good hand with needle and thread making nice tight stiches will leave a nice scar to impress the gals. By gawd how it strings but I grind my teeth trying to make no sound some of the boys are watching seeing how it take it, respect is earned. Everyone takes the deaths hard, seems the young Vaquero killed was one of Salvador's nephews Joe was a well respected hard working cowboy who rode for the brand, Triple Creek's death I think must hit Smoke and Mr. Sam hard they had been riding together and had crossed many rivers together, damn it to hell. Me, Billy and a couple boys got the shovels and begin to dig the graves talk is quiet and low like being in church it sure does make a body think of how quick death can find you on the trail, them men including myself are getting tough and a bit mean everyman in his heart swears to get this herd through not for the owners but the damn fine men we leave buried in a vast lonely lands sadly these brave men will have no grave markers but will live as long as the outfit lives.

Smoke decides to take a day off to get things back in order tend to our wounds, equipment and weapons, breakfast is biscuits bacon and coffee and the coffee taste damn fine this morning nothing like escaping extreme danger to begin to learn to appreciate the small things in life, like a good Cuban cigar or a fine cup of coffee. My cheek stings like hornets are at it but Mr. Sam did I nice job stitching me up but with lots to do I keep busy and try not concentrate on it, Smoke and Salvador come over to where I repairing some of the chuckwagons leather harness damaged in the run. Salvador smiling gives me a playful punch in the shoulder which knocks me back about 3 feet, damn the big man has power in him both older men chuckle at my expense Smoke does the talking, "Jim lad Cookie tells us you did some real good work during the run seems you are getting pretty handy with that hogleg Mr. Sam says it was a hell of a fine shot to put that Kiowa under. We just make a cowboy of you yet but now I am going to have you to dig deep and get iron on iron hard besides losing 3 men the Bundy boys lit out during the fighting taking 6 horses with them, we are shorthanded every man will have to give his all then give some more, are you with us Jim lad?" "Boss I will damn well will be with you when getting to Dodge city and if I ain't there I died, you tell me what needs doing and point me to er, Pa always told me always finish what you start no matter how difficult lots of men talk a good game but most are talkers no doers and talk is cheap."

The boss was not kidding the next 10 days moving the herd was a nightmare, be lucky to get 3 hours a night, long hours in the saddle and lack of sleep are grinding me down tempers are getting short, Smoke and Salvador are everywhere keeping the men awake urging them on. We move at a good pace and will be in Kansas soon then should be smooth sailing into Dodge, but the man working the hardest is Mr. Sam, being short handed he no longer has a helper, Smoke told him keep the coffee on and the meals simple and break out the jerky men can eat in the saddle. I curse the Bundy cousins for their disloyal and cowardly departure and swear I catch up with them it is going to be hot lead and gun smoke. I am not alone in my thinking Smoke hates quitters and knows their 2 guns might have meant fewer of are men going under, I a sure glad Smoke ain't coming for me, if them Bundy boys are smart they will not stop running until they get to Canada.

A few days later we enter Kansas we still have a fair piece to travel but the worst is past us and with luck we can be in Dodge city in 7 to 10 day, Smoke calls Billy and I over and sends us out scouting for water or signs of other herds the first to arrive get the best grass to fatten up the beeves. The owners will want them fat and sassy for the cattle buyers, about 2 miles in front of the herd we come over a small rise and find 8 hard looking men waiting for us and be damned if 2 of them were Chet and Elmer Bundy both looking right smug. A man sits his horse just a bit in front of the others he will be the leader and mouth piece, I take the leather thong off the hammer of my.45 Billy does the same, damn this could get ugly. The leader has a scar and a brown leather patch over his left eye his good eye shining black with malice a cruel smile comes to his face just before he speaks." Howdy boys welcome to Kansas you boys must be with that cattle outfit we have been waiting for been watching your dust for days, this here is my land so you tell your boss the toll for using my land is 2 dollars a cow I figure 1600 should about cover it if you don't pay up there will be Double M cattle spread out all over the Kansas plains now that's a fair deal."

I look to Billy he is eager and ready I look back at old one eye, "Mr. first off I got to say you keep poor company both those Bundy boys are pure pond scum and I figure you should talk to the boss and I will have him here directly. But if you men start anything now matter how the chips fall you and Chet Bundy will not live to spend the money now don't get jumpy I am going to take out my smokewagon." Slowly I take up the Schofield and then point it at the sky I then fire 3 shots into the air 3 shots means trouble come a running, I lower my gun open the cylinder and replace the 3 spent shells keeping my eyes locked on a nervous looking Chet Bundy. Within a few minutes we can see Smoke and Salvador riding towards us and not sparing the spurs, both men pull their horses sharply covering old one eye and his pack of coyotes with thick dust, Smoke immediately takes control of the situation, "So boys what's going on here and why are you men not looking for water not chatting the day away with these assholes," I tell the boss about the toll and the threat to stampede and scatter the herd, and I also tell him if it comes to shooting Chet is my meat. Smoke gives off one of his rare smiles this is for those know him is when he is at his most dangerous, "Damn fine bluff there cyclops but before I left Texas I checked the maps and this strip of land is government owned and we are free to travel it so there will be no gold eagles just chucks of hot lead I do not bluff so when I say I will hunt down and kill every one of you, I will, there is no place you will ever be safe, my name is Smoke Kellerman I ramrod this outfit and if I say it I mean it- sure as shooting."

I cannot help but smile at the Jayhawkers reaction when they heard who they were messing with Smoke Kellerman one of the deadliest men in the west with many close friends just as tough then in a blink of an eye the world turns to chaos blood and death. One of the Kansas boys makes his last mistake pulls his gun and lets loose, I draw lining up Chet but Elmer gets in the way and takes the lead meant for his cousin, all goes quiet 5 dead men lay motionless on the ground their blood soaking into the dry dirt. Shit that damn Chet has the luck I watch as him and a couple riders ride away like the devil is on their tails I look to Elmer he has made his last ride and good riddance, Smoke is looking around to make sure all his boys are ok. "Jim you and Billy did a mans job of it today, you kept calm in a tough spot now do you 2 badasses can get on with your work and scout out some water them cow critters are thirsty again, we will take care of things here, now get."

Word must have gotten out that Smoke Kellerman and his Texas boys are a tough crowd and will not tolerate any interference for we had no more trouble from Jayhawkers before I know it we are only 2 days out from the stockyards in Dodge city, hot damn looks like I am going to make it and have a bath and sit at a table for supper with a nice chuck of change after Smoke sells the cattle, damn it is a nice day.

CHAPTER 7

DODGE CITY

The Boss stops the herd just over 2 miles from Dodge there is good grass and water here and they will be easy to manage and not stray, the boys are eager to get to town but a few have to stay back, Billy and I said we could wait and go in later, Mr. Sam stayed and a couple Vaqueros to care for the horse herd we watch as the boys dash out of camp whooping their fool heads off. I am a bit disappointed but do not mind that much never cared for the red eye whiskey I like a cold beer now and again and no spoiled doves for me women still scare me more than river crossings. Next morning some sorry looking cowboys ride back into camp, from the black eyes and skinned knuckles looks like they had themselves a wild night. They told us Smoke says come on in and meet him at the Cattlemen's club to get paid, we did not have to be told twice running we bounce ourselves into our saddles and ride hell for leather to the most famous city in the west.

When we enter the Cattlemen's Club Smoke is behind a desk handing out brown enveloped to the riders in line Billy and I join the line and wait our turn, when my turn comes Smoke smiles and hands me my envelope telling me there is 200 dollars a 50 dollar bonus for each man the cattle sold better than expected, damn 200 dollars I never thought I would see this much money. Before I leave Smoke tells me to meet him at the Marshals office in a couple hours someone he wants me to meet. I tell Billy I am for a bath haircut and getting some new duds mine are worn the fabric so thin you can almost read through it, Billy says he is going to have a few drinks with the boys but will catch up for supper.

I head directly to the general store to get my new cloths before I go over to the bathhouse, entering the aromas of leather, spices, gun oil fill the air I take a deep breath enjoying the pleasantness of it all. It costs me dear but I leave the store with new high top leather boots, a couple cotton checkered shirts and corduroy pants, 2 pairs of long johns, and a black Stetson with a thin leather headband, with a couple of long bandanas and a leather vest completes my shopping spree and I still got over 140 dollars left now for that bath.

I stand in front of a big window admiring myself but looking back at me now is a man where only a short while back a boy stood I cannot help feeling a sense of pride, I remember I am to get over to the Marshal's office to meet up with Smoke. The door is open so I step in and there standing big as life is none other than Wild Bill himself no mistaking that long hair grey eyes and the 2 pistols tucked into red sash, "Jim lad I would like you to meet a friend of mine and the Marshal here in Dodge city Mr. James Hickok better know as Wild Bill, James this here is Jim Thorton he is Don Thorton's boy and is already making his own trails like his father." Wild Bill extends his hand in friendship his grip firm is hands dry and cool, "Pleased to meet you Jim I knew your Pa a good man and a damn fine fighting man, looks like you are shaping up and ready to make your own tracks." "Now for the real reason we had you come over is to warn you Chet Bundy is in town and is telling anyone who will lesson he aims to kill you and will shoot you on sight, I would like to throw his sorry ass in jail but he ain't broke no town laws.

Smoke tells me are no trouble maker and do look for trouble but get yourself ready son that son of a bitch means to take your life, if it comes to shooting do not worry about fast make sure your first shot hits hard and true even if it means taking one, well let's hope it does not come to that. "Well you boys will have to excuse me I have to make my rounds if you are looking for some good home cooking Miss Martha's eatery is the best in town with the best coffee see you boys later for a drink, Adios."

Smoke says we got time for a quick beer before supper so we head over to the long Branch saloon to have a quick beer and see how the crew is making out, the tables are all full so we make our way to the end of the bar, I look down the to the far end into the eyes of Chet Bundy there is blood in his eye I know he wants me gut shot and bleeding out on the sawdust wooden floor. "Thorton you killed my cousin Elmer and for that I aim to kill you right here and now you son of a bitch, you ready to die boy." I take a second before answering the challenge, "Chet you sure do talk big for a man who ran from a battle when his crew needed him, I was trying to kill you but you dumb cousin got in the way I recon to correct that mistake right now come out from behind the bar and let's see if you are a gun thrower or just brag, so you ready asshole time for you to die."

Men back away from the bar, Smoke puts his hand on my shoulder and reminds me what the great Marshal said and to kill that piece of wasted skin and be done with it, we both move out from our opposite ends of the long bar we now stand facing each other about 40 feet apart I then fall into the gunfighter stance Pa taught me and watch Chet's eyes. He blinks and grabs for his colt.45 as his hand grabs the handle of his gun the Schofield bucks and barks twice and my hot lead smashes into Chet's chest the bullets not more than 2 inches apart, the outlaw looks at me in disbelief he did not even clear his gun from its holster. Slowly and whimpering he falls to his knees with one last groan he falls on his face first dead and gone, Adios asshole. Marshal Hickok hearing the shooting enters the saloon holding a gun in each hand I put my gun back in the holster and remove my gun belt placing it on the bar and wait to see what will happen next. Hickok talks to Smoke and a few of the other men in the bar then announces in a loud tone that it was a fair fight and no further action will be taken and then tells the swamper to go get the undertaker and get this piece of filth out of the bar.

I then strap my gunbelt back around my waste, men now crowd around me to congratulate me and buy me drinks, I feel I am being smothered and am having a hard time breathing, Billy forces himself through the crowd and stands beside me. I then feel a ham sized ham on my shoulder and see Salvador standing there I follow close as he breaks for the door men wisely step aside and let us pass once out into the open air I notice my hands are still shaking a bit. Well gunfight or not I aim to have a home cooked meal at Miss Martha's before I head back to camp, I have had enough of town I will make one last stop and get a good supply of cigars, riding back gives me time to think I say to myself with pride I ride for Smoke Kellerman and the Double M ranch, I am a cowboy and I know now what it truly means to ride for the brand.

LOYALTY MEANS NOTHING UNLESS AT ITS HEART
THE ABSOLUTE PRINCIPLE OF SELF-SACRIFICE-
WOODROW T WILSON

STORY 4

ALWAYS FINISH
WHAT YOU START

CHAPTER 1

WHEN THERE IA NO ONE ELSE

The year is 1813 Mrs. Laura Secord is a Loyalist married to Sgt. James Secord, a remarkable woman who went to the battlefield to retrieve her wounded husband and bring him home to tend his wounds. The Secord's live in Queenston which is occupied by the Americans with some American Officers billeted in the Secord home. One evening Mrs. Secord overhears that the Americans are planning a surprise attack on the Outpost at Beaver Dams commanded by Lieutenant James Fitzgibbon, with here husband recovering and unable to travel there was no one else so this brave and determined on herself to make the 20 mile journey to warn Fitzgibbon of the enemies intention.

Now 20 miles might not seem a long distance but the ground she had to cover is extremely hilly, rocky and with dense bush and trees making travel not only extremely difficult but with slippery rock surfaces one misstep could lead to disaster and being stranded helpless in the vast wilderness. Mrs. Secord knew there was many scouts and enemy sentries between her and the outpost and wisely took a circular route around in danger every minute she came very close to being caught by an American patrol, she knew if captured she would be shot as a spy.

Mrs. Secord did with help from some friendly Natives got to Fitzgibbon in time and the American attack failed, if Mrs. Secord had given up North America could look much different today. It is the Same with Kit Carson making super human rides in order to bring New Mexico into the United States, and there have been so many who stepped forward when they were needed most, so never start anything you don't aim on finishing.

The year is 1877 Lynne Bridger is hiding and frightened, from her secret spot she can hear the Utes destroying her little home, damn them her husband Sam Bridger put his hearts blood sweat and tears into making her a home she now hears another group of riders joins the Ute warriors it is then she hears a white mans voice, "Colorow my friend it is good we meet again it is time to gather your men for the attack on Fort Fred Steele me and my men will meet you at the Big Stones in 5 days, now everyone in the fort must be killed then you can have everything the guns ammunition horses food crazy water but we are taking the gold is that understood my Ute Brother." Colorow is also known as Colorado by many wants very badly what treasures the fort holds and what does he care for gold can not eat it but with the guns and horses he will be able to drive all the white eyes out of his land. "Manson yes we have a deal I do not speak with forked tongue as the whites, we will do as you ask but after we have destroyed the fort and killed its soldiers you will have only 2 days to get out of Ute country because very soon all the whites will have gone or will be killed. It will be life as back to the old ways you have the word of Colorado, we will be at Big Stones when you say we go now have far to travel, remember white man no tricks"

The man Manson replies it will be as he says the fort will only have a few men and with surprise can be taken easily and he was looking forward to the battle and treasure to follow the riders depart without another word. Lynne can feel herself shaking she wants to cry or scream but there may still be a few Ute's lingering going through the scraps of was just a few minutes ago her home, she knows she has to wait. Damn that Husband of hers out scouting for the Army but she is thankful Sam would have fought brave but would be dead and cold by now, she listens closely for at least 20 minutes not a sound but the fire can be heard slowly with a small prayer she crawls from her hole. Her husband Sam was a far thinking and skilled plainsman, he has planned ahead in case of attack she is alive because of it but now she must see what she can salvage and get to the fort and warn Major Kendall. Mrs. Bridger knows the country almost as good as Sam and knows it is 70 miles of pure hell from the ranch to Fort Fred Steele and if that is not enough every Ute warrior is out with war paint and sharp knives looking for scalps her blond hair would be highly prized hanging from a coup stick or war lance.

Lynne takes a quick look to the burning house and barn and knows immediately the hungry fires will devour everything but she has herself a damn smart man without a look back she walks behind the burning buildings into the rocks and crevices she walks through the twists and turns for no more than 10 minutes before it opens to reveal a small hidden meadow now more than 200 yards wide with a narrow clear water stream and some sweet tall green grass. Sam with foresight knew when he found this place it was perfect for storing emergency supplies but most important is our appaloosa gelding Charger which Sam hid knowing without a horse in this country you are up against it, Charger is one hell of a horse not tall no more than 5 and a half hands but solid strong legs got good speed but it is his bottom that makes him a great horse no horse in Wyoming can stay with him. Over a days travel, he takes it and then wants more she is saddened by the thought of the brutality she would have to put her very much love horse through but peoples lives are on the line. In this dry and dangerous country it is easy to stick out but not the case with the Appy almost a solid light grey coat and a white face and nose blends into the landscape avoiding detection and endurance will be the keys to survival on this ride.

Horses are herding animals and if left alone to long can go loco so Sam brought in a goat named Butthead and a small cart pony named Daisy and he took just fine to their company they are walk up to great her. Charger nuzzles his velvet nose on my face and neck she talks to him soft and quiet for a moment she wavers thinking of what brutality she must put her beautiful and loyal horse through, she puts her forehead on hers on his and cries for a couple minutes. Snapping out of it quickly she is ashamed of her weakness from now until the fort it will be iron on iron hard and mule stubborn she goes and opens the shed door first thing she sees is the light cavalry saddle, saddle blanket and bridle, in the lather rifle scabbard was a Henry level action 44.40 rifle that holds 16 bullets. Lynne smiles because the Henry is her favorite rifle, light, fast lever action, accurate and reliable weapon. Sam planned well there was 2 canteens, extra bullets, a beat-up old straw hat to keep the sun from frying her brain like an egg. The last items she gathers up are a tightly wrapped package of rawhide tough buffalo jerky and a large serious looking folding knife with a 6 inch blade and Sam likes his knives sharp always tells her it's the dull knives that cut you, she hides the knife in her skirt, Lynne knows the knife is her last line of defence but in reality it is for her to cut her throat and end her life before the Utes can take her for their amusement.

Charger knows he is going travelling and is pawing the ground with a front hoof snorting raring to go, Lynne throws the saddle and gear on him makes sure the saddle bags and rifle boot are tie on tight and secure satisfied she has all she needs for the trip the last thing she does is take Charger to the water the horse drinks as she fills her canteens. The water is teeth hurting cold tasting of minerals then she drinks all the water she can take her man says water is best on the inside. Water in the dry semi desert of Wyoming is scarce Sam always wanted her to know the ways of the land in case he was not there for her one of his teaching is in dry country the best place for water is inside you and watch for bees or certain animals that stay close to water, reaching over she grabs Chargers reins and leads the horse out of the small hidden valley.

CHAPTER 2

INTO THE VALLEY OF THE SHADOW

Once out of the rocks and on flat ground she climbs up into the hurricane deck and as she expected old Charger not ridden for a spell is a bit rank and kicks his heels up a bit, Lynne being a fine horsewoman sticks to the saddle like glue, it is an old game with the 2, the grey horse settles down and Lynne points him east towards Fort Fred Steele. It is getting late in the day they will run a ground eating trot until it is to dark to travel, Charger has a beautiful smooth gait and being fresh they got some miles in before they and had to find a hole to hide in for a few hours rest, tomorrow will be a hard brutal day for them both. Once Charger is unsaddled, she lets the horse loose, Charger does not need tying he will never stray far from Lynne and will warn her of trouble better than any guard dog. It has been a long day of violence and loss she is weary but must be careful not oversleep 2 hours at the most her eyes grow heavy and get hard to keep open before she drifts off she snaps open the long bladed folding knife and holds on to it tightly even after she falls asleep.

A young Ute warrior named Blue Fox smiles in the darkness, what luck a lone woman and a most beautiful horse he will kill the woman and take the horse a horse as great as this will make him big in the eyes of the other warriors. He is not far from the woman but now he must crawl putting his knife between his teeth he moves slowly with stealth and without sound works slowly towards his sleeping prey. What the young Ute did not count on was Charger just before he is within striking distance the horse lets out a scream of danger, he sees the woman move and rushes her. Lynn sits up quickly just in time to see a black ghost coming at her fast the ghost leaps to jump on her, Lynn strikes blindly upwards and feels the long razor sharp blade cut into the Indian's stomach going under the rib cage cutting open her attackers heart the now dead Ute now lays on top of her making it difficult for her to breath. Getting up she nearly panics unable to push the dead weight off her breath coming in gasps. With one last heave she manages to free herself she looks on in shock at the unmoving black ghost, blood covers her she can feel it cooling and getting sticky on her skin her stomach sours at the thought of what she had just done and what little she had in her stomach came up and then the dry heaves feeling weak she goes to her knees.

The pre dawn grey of morning looms in the eastern sky as much as she hates to use the water she washes the blood off her hands and knife, then cupping her hand filling it with water she gives the horse a drink, he will need it more than her she then takes a long drink and saddles up her resolve stronger after surviving the attack, today they had to make many miles with a gentle kick in the ribs Charger takes off like shot it thrills her to feel the power of this wonderful animal. When it is light enough Lynne checks herself over she sees her dress and arms covered in dried blood, a lot of blood her attacker bled out quick, she lets Charger have his head for a couple miles then brings him back into a trot this is how they would travel today, best way to make miles and still have Charger ready to run if spotted by the Utes.

Lynne constantly watches the horizon for movement as she rides she thinks back to when she first met Sam in St Louis the moment she saw the big tall confident mans man she fell in love and as fate would have it he fell just as hard for her. Back then her family were part of the snob bunch, poor people who only had money. She thinks back on how golden her hair was, her eyes pools of blue her skin milk white and flawless, with a grimace she realizes her once gold hair has faded to a straw colour her eyes paled with crows feet around her eyes from the glaring sun, her exposed skin tanned dark, she looks at her hands still slim but now rough from work needed doing by a ranch woman. One thing she knew for sure is she never regretted for a minute coming to the wilds of Wyoming with Sam and she knows she will survive cause no damn Utes are going to keep her from her man-sure as shooting.

Checking her back trail Lynne sees 2 Utes giving chase pushing their horses hard to catch her, she presses her straw hat down firmly and then with a Sioux war cry she puts Charger into a full out run the warriors horse are no match and fall quickly behind Lynn pulls the horse back a little but still running fast soon the Indians were out of sight, Lynne takes a deep breath and just calming down when a bullet passes close to her head so close it sounded like a bee buzzing by her ear, damn 3 more warriors are coming at her from the left she puts Charger into a run and pulls the henry rifle from the boot. Charger still has some bottom left but in an instant everything changes Chargers front left leg hits a hole and he goes down throwing Lyn from the saddle, clinging tightly to her rifle she tries her best to roll with the fall, she hits hard but knowing she has no time to hesitate she goes to one knee puts the rifle to her shoulder finds her target takes a small breath and holds it the rifle bucks and a Ute brave falls from his horse quickly Lynne jacks another round into the rifle they are almost on her now, she fires taking out a second warrior but has to roll quickly out of the way of a Ute spear. Missing the Ute tries to turn his horse when a 44.40 chunk of hot lead takes out his spine, she looks around quickly for any further danger but all three men are dead.

A numbness of fear now floods though her as she goes over to Charger praying he be alright, but luck is still riding with her the horse is no worse for wear, patting the horses neck she thanks the saints, taking a minute she reloads the henry rifle before putting it back in the boot. Red hot pain now assaults in her legs and left shoulder, looking herself over she finds the fall took its toll both knees were badly scraped as well as her upper left arm. There is no way to clean the wounds only thing Lynne can to is dig deep within herself to find another level of strength she cannot help but cry out as she places her battered body back in the saddle. She sits motionless for a moment her head down, Charger is getting restless tossing his big head back and forth then a smile comes to her lips remembering her mans prayer, "Yea though I walk through the valley of the shadow of death I fear no evil for I am the meanest son of a bitch in the valley", gritting her teeth she smiles and continues on her mission.

"Officer of the guard rider approaching looks be a lone woman she appears injured sir and her horse looks plum wore out." The young officer climbs up to the parapet and immediately orders 2 riders to bring her in and to go gentle, when the main gate is opened 2 mounted soldiers ride hell bent for leather to retrieve to woman. Lynne is not sure if she can trust her eyes can it be she made it please let it be so, she can barely keep in the saddle she tells herself just to hang on a bit longer she has to talk to the Commander immediately she is not even sure what day it is. The riders meet up with her a Sgt with a soft voice tells her it is ok and she is safe now just hold on and they would lead her in, in a dry raspy voice tells the soldiers she must see Major Kendall at once it is most urgent.

Major Thomas Kendall Commander of Fort Fred Steele is horrified by the appearance of his friend Lynne Bridger, Sam and him go way back, it is Thomas who introduced Lynne and Sam his wife Martha and Lynne were at school together and are very close. The Major calls for the Sgt Major to fetch the doctor and his wife on the double, the Sgt Major barks at a couple troopers and they take off at the double, double time. The riders are now gently and tenderly helping the semi conscious Mrs. Bridger into the Majors office, the Doctor and Mrs. Kendall arrive almost at the same time Martha lets out a cry filled with despair and fear then rushes to her friend. The Sgt major brings in a pitcher of cold well water and fills a glass for Lynne, she thanks him with a weak smile, the doctor orders clean hot water and begins to tend to the tired woman's wounds, never in her life had water tasted to so good, clearing her throat she tells Thomas to pour her a large glass of the Irish whiskey he has in his desk. "Thomas I am nearly done in I need the whiskey to get through what I have to say, a horrible evil is coming for us Major, now let's have that drink." Thomas smiles at his friend soft as goose down hard as wang leather, he hands her a big double shot of whisky which she knocks back in 2 quick drinks she shudders as the fiery liquid hits her empty stomach like a sledgehammer. "Major Kendall the Utes attacked our ranch burnt the house and barn stole the livestock I was able to make it to the hideout Sam had set up and they did not find me but while the devils were destroying my home. Some white men rode in and had a meeting with the Utes, I heard a man named Manson planning the assault on the fort, Colorado and his warriors are to attack and kill every living soul in the fort and they can have everything but the gold I do not know how many renegades there are with Manson but there are more than enough Utes to go around. They are meeting at Big Rocks and going to attack Friday morning I have lost track of the days but I know you have little time to prepare, Thomas they plan to kill everyone that means the women and children we can not let that happen."

Major Kendall curses then apologizes to the ladies, "That damn Manson formally Captain Chance Manson, thief and deserter on an occasion a few months back military payrolls being slow had a double pay come in the Captain was the Pay Officer at the time, in the morning the troops line up for pay parade only to find their pay master went over the hill with their money and has not been seen since. I have no idea how he learned of the gold, we are holding gold bullion worth more than 200 thousand dollars, we are holding it for Wells Fargo to pick it up, damn." The Major looks to his injured friend to find her asleep the Doc gave her a sedative better if she were not awake when he cleaned the rashes, Mrs. Kendall orders a stretcher and tells the Doctor she is taking Lynne to her house the men have work to do. The Major orders Officers call and all NCO'S report to him at once, time for war talk.

CHAPTER 3

I HAVE NOT FINISHED

Lynne wakes late that night a lamp is lit casting shadows in the small room she turns her head and smiles weakly as she sees her dear friend Martha sleeping in the rocking chair without thinking she goes to move red intense pain shoots through her she quickly falls back breathing deeply. The noise stirs Martha awake the women smile at each other with genuine affection of long time friends Martha takes Lynne's hand and tells her to lay back then asks if she needs anything. "My dear Martha I could use some water my throat is parched my meeting with Thomas is a bit hazy is he aware of the upcoming attack how much time do we have Martha?" "Lynne honey he knows and is preparing this is not his first Indian fight him and your Sam have been in some tough scraps, the only problem is the post is seriously undermanned at most he has 20 men to man the walls, but he is a fighter and survivor I put my trust in him we have one full day." "Martha you tell Thomas that when the time comes I will be on the wall with my Henry and I will need cartridges, I think I will try to sleep a bit more, it is good we are together now it is as it should be."

Major Kendall chews on his lit cigar as he briefs the officers no panic in his voice appearing cool as a mountain stream, being an experienced and tested warrior he knows the reality that the fort and its people are in real danger but one thing to his advantage and something Manson has no way of knowing that last supply train brought in 2 two 12 pounder mountain howitzers, shells and a 8 man crew to man the big guns. "Gunnery Sgt. Taylor I believe is they are coming from the Big Rocks they plan on hitting us at first light head on hit us like a huge wave, I want your guns moved forward but out of sight ready to be rolled forward ready to fire in under a minute. Leave the solid shot out and use only cannister we have to have them in close and if we do not have cannister go to the blacksmith and get all the nails and rough metal you will only fire by my order do you understand Gunnery Sgt?" Sgt. Taylor is an old salt and knew his job his men were more than ready and looking for a fight, he tells the Major that they have 12 loads of nasty canister the new shells are much improved and much more effective in making huge holes in the enemies lines and his men are ready and they would have the guns in place within hours and no questions.

The Major smiles appreciating the fact the Sgt. knows his job and they are lucky to have him and his men, may make the difference, "Thank you Gunnery Sgt., report back to me when you have your artillery in place, gentlemen make no doubt about it we are not only in for the fight for our lives but the lives of every woman and child at the post. The cowardly deserter Manson has gathered white renegades and joined with Colorado and the Utes we could be facing as many as 300 or more of the enemy Sgt. Major how many men can we get on the wall and I mean every loving man except the Doctor?" the Sgt Major was prepared for the question answering that there were 32 men to man the walls, the number hits the Major almost like a slap so few long odds at near 10 to one, damn that Manson. The Major announces "The Sgt Major will be my second in command and oversee the many and placement of the men on the wall, when he speaks he is speaking for me rank be damned now there is much to be done we only have the rest of today and tomorrow to prepare, Sgt Major release Trooper Brannon from the guardhouse and have him report to me immediately, dismissed gentlemen", the room comes to attention all saluting before exiting the Commanders office.

Formally Sgt Rock Brannon now Trooper Brannon after a payday adventure of drinking and a little knuckle and skull fun with some of the boys has landed him in the guardhouse, but the major let him off fairly lightly 10 days in the digger and busted down to Trooper. This does not worry rock at all he hads been busted so many times he has his own seamstress sewing on and removing chevrons. Rock is a big man at 6 foot 2 and wide across the shoulders tough as they come between the war and the Indian fighting has survived 18 hard fought battles. The Trooper marches into the Majors office and snaps to perfect attention giving the Commander a sharp salute, the Major tells him to stand easy then tells the Trooper to close the door then pulls his bottle of Irish out of the drawer and pours each of them a drink. "Rock sit and have a taste of the Irish with me I have a tough job for you and you are going to hate me for it but you are the only man I know strong enough for what may you may have to do, we been together a long while now Rock no man I trust more you and old knot head Sam, I am placing my wife and Mrs. Bridger in your hands and under your protection until after the battle is fought and won." "You are to aid the women in every way possible but if things go bad and get through the gates and there is no way out, DAMN, DAMN IT TO HELL, you know what you must do the women cannot be alive when the Utes get to them, I know it is a hell of a thing to ask Rock and it is not an order it is a favour for an old friend and comrade, here have another shot, I need your answer Pard and I need it now."

Trooper Rock Brannon knocks back the breath taking brew in one gulp and slams his glass to the table near breaking it, "Now Tom Lad do not fret I will look after the lasses to my last breath I will do as you ask out of love for you and Martha and Lynne, is sure wish Sam was here he is worth 4 soldiers fear not Boss if there is life there is hope. We are far from under the flowers now with the Majors permission I need to prepare", the 2 old soldiers do not salute on parting but shake hands and wishing each other luck. Rock heads to the barracks there he changes into a clean uniform straps a gun belt around his waist in its holster a long barrelled army .45 colt revolver, from the deer horn rack above his bed he takes down his Winchester level action rifle, he stuffs extra cartridges in his pockets grabs his canteen and makes a beeline to the Majors house and his charges.

Lynne hears someone talking with Martha at the front door then a few seconds a big man fills the doorway recognizing the soldier she smiles, "Rock you big lug it is so good to see you, I see you got busted down again, you and that damn Irish thirst, now what brings you by old friend." Rock told her everything but the likely outcome but he knew these women are now western clean through and know why Trooper Brannon is wearing a sidearm. The Trooper now at her beck and call he is at the ladies beck and call asks for is her rifle and a gun cleaning kit and go to the hospital and see if they have a set of crutches lastly she asks the Trooper to pick up a 12 gauge double barrelled sawed off shotgun for Martha, smiling Brannon heads off to run his errands.

After Rock leaves Lynne unloads the Henry rifle she carefully cleans and lightly oils the weapon satisfied she reloads the rifle and places it beside the bed, the rest of the day is a bit fuzzy she fades in and out her body fighting its injuries. Rock returns with both crutches and shotgun, her eyes close and do not open until the sun coming in the lone window wakes her, her first thought it is the last day and she has to move she calls for the big Trooper. Rock and Martha did there best to keep her resting in bed but they both knew it was a losing battle, as gently as possible Rock helps Lynne off the bed he can almost taste her pain as sweat pops out on her forehead her teeth grinding so not to scream. Now with the crutches under her arms she finds although it hurts like hellfire she can move her legs but very slowly, Martha then tells the Trooper to go around to the married quarters and ask the ladies to come here to the house as soon as they are able and do not bring the children, with a mock salute he is off and running once more. Lynne hobbles out to the small veranda and sits on an old wooden chair waiting impatiently for the soldier's wives to arrive.

Women slowly begin to arrive uncertainty and fear showing on their faces, but army wives are on the most times tougher than their husband soldiers, there were faint of heart at this post Martha calls for quiet and begins to speak. "Ladies I asked you here today to tell you exactly what our situation is and ask for your help, this Lady sitting is my friend Lynne Bridger wife of the scout Sam Bridger, Lynne's ranch was looted and burned by the Utes then discovered that a white renegade named Manson and his bunch are going to attack the fort tomorrow morning. Lynne made a ride through hell and killed 4 Utes getting word to the Commander I think it is best you hear what she heard from her own lips and then decisions will be made. Lynne looks over the group of women there is no panic no fussing she suddenly felt a certain pride and connection with these hard-living women.

"Morning ladies there is no way to sugar coat it so going to fire from the shoulder tomorrow morning there are going to be about 300 Ute warriors and white renegades attacking their intention is to take all the fort has to give and I heard this very clearly from the renegade leader that every man woman and child is to be killed so in a nutshell if they get through the gates we all die and that means your children slaves or dead. "I told the Major that me and my henry rifle will be on wall my dear friend Martha will be at my shoulder, what we are asking is if you can shoot a gun we can use your help defending the fort and if not can load for the shooters. "Ladies I am not going to let them kill me they will have to fight me for that and I don't plan on giving it up easy some of those heathens are crossing over with me, it really is simple ladies you fight or you and your children are slaughtered. You must decide quickly if you need a weapon or ammunition see trooper Brannon, I recon about time to teach them pesky Utes that they picked the wrong damn outpost to attack that is all I have to say, good luck to you all."

Major Kendall stands on the parapet in the pre dawn light the gunnery crews are in place and the men are posted along the walls for the best defence they could with their limited numbers, behind him he hears a racket and sees Trooper Brannon leading his Wife, Lynne and 12 women all armed but 2 he comes rushing down the stairs, "Trooper Brannon just what the hell do you think you and these women are doing, morning is coming soon and it is going to get real hot up on that wall." Before poor old Rock could respond Martha jumps in with a no nonsense tone, "Major Kendall I have no desire to be slaughtered like a sheep if I am going to die it will be standing with my husband now if you please honey could you assign the ladies their places their firing positions." In exasperation the Major slams his battered campaign hat against his leg and calls for the Sgt Major to get the women settled quickly the sun will be up soon. Rock picks up Lynne like a child and carries her up the stairs and places her close to the Major and Martha and settles in right beside her the Major orders everyone down out of sight he wants the enemy to think they are attacking a sleepy fort, Lynne and Rock talk about Sam and the hell they used to raise this helped Lynne for she is frightened even more frightened than on the hard ride, waiting is always the hard part.

The sun finally breaks over the eastern hills a blinding morning light washes over the fort, the defenders can now hear the thunder of hundreds of horses and wars cries shatter the morning still, the Major tells everyone to stay down and the gun crew to get ready no one is to fire until he gives the order then pour it to them. Wising everyone good luck he kisses Martha then draws his saber from its scabbard, raising his sword high in the air he orders the gunnery crew into position and the riflemen and women to stand and take aim. Lynne puts her front site on a white renegade in a fringe jacket and holds her breath.

"FIRE"

REGRET IS NOT WHEN YOU COULD NOT FINISH WHAT YOU STARTED BUT REGRET IS WHEN YOU DO NOT START WHAT YOU COULD HSAVE FINISHED-APOORVE DUBEY

STORY 5

TALK LESS SAY MORE

CHAPTER 1

THE NEW MAN

I stand beside Pa watching a lone rider slowly riding towards were we are standing in front of our small but very well built ranch house out here in the wilds of New Mexico about 12 miles from the town of Las Cruces, ours is just a small spread compared to the ranches along our borders. Pa was a man who likes to grow things we have a few cattle mostly for food but it is the fruit trees and vegetables Pa likes most, unlike most ranches we keep laying hens, a few pigs and a good Jersey cow for milk and butter, we lived modest but had much and are thankful. The Rider rides into the yard slow not to raise dust and pulls up and sits quiet with a bit of a smile waits to be invited down, Pa and I look him over, appears to be tall man with long riders legs and wide shoulders his cloths are not new but good quality range clothes a beat up black Stetson hat with high top leather riding boots, shit kickers as we call them out here. Pleasant looking in some ways average until you look into his blazing green eyes that seem to look right through a man into his soul. The stranger has a scar on his left cheek from what I figure is a knife or arrow, then I notice to my surprise he is not wearing a six gun, rare out here but did have a damn fine 44.40 Winchester 73 in his rifle scabbard. You can tell a lot about a man about the horse he rides Pa is always saying outlaws and lawmen always have the best horse so to get out of trouble faster than they get in. The strangers horse is the most beautiful horse I ever saw a pure Saddlebred standing over 16 hands his coat a light tan with a white spot on his forehead and a white lone running down his nose, Pa breaks the silence.

"Howdy Stranger my name is Jason Flynn and this my boy Nathen we call him Nat so what can we do for you looks like you come a fair piece?" Smiling the rider answers Pa, "Howdy hunting job if you got one if not would be obliged if can water old Ten-Ten here and maybe a coffee if it is on, most folks just call me Wade." Pa tells Wade to light and he is welcome to use the water trough, as for the job they would have a civilized talk over coffee and a smoke, he sends me to the house to ask Ma to put the coffee on. Pa tells Wade to tie up his horse on the shade and come over to the bench that he had made for eating or talking in the shade of a big live oak. I can hear the men talking in low tones as I wait to help Ma carry the coffee out and hot damn she is putting out the cookies, Ma bakes the best cookies in New Mexico, when all is ready I grab the big wood tray and Ma carries the big coffee pot out to the men.

When Wade sees Ma come from the house he quickly gets to his feet and takes off his hat, the bright sun makes her red hair look like liquid fire shimmering her green eyes smiling at the gesture, Pa wisely jumps to his feet as well and introduces Ma to Wade. "Wade this here is my better Half Cara my sweet Irish lass and fiery as her red hair, Cara, Wade is looking for work how about you and Nat join us for coffee and we will talk the matter over." Ma sits across from Wade giving him a good look over, then smiles, "Welcome Wade please call me Cara, need a change from Ma, there is no hiding the smell of peat on you where were your family from before the left the emerald isle." There is no fooling you Cara a long while Back my family lived in Castlebar in Mayo county, my Grandfather was soldier and mercenary when he had made his nest egg he grabbed the most beautiful gal in Ireland and came across the big pond now here I am living in a new open country always something new to see or challenge, the west has me hooked like a trout." Ma said the boys could smoke Wade takes a couple black thin Mexican cigars from his pocket and offers one to Pa who smiles happily accepts, Ma not asking told Wade he would be staying for supper then after eating they will talk about the job, but if he was smart he would be heading out quick in the morning, Wade just gives her an impish grin and wink but says nothing.

The harsh thick smoke from the cigars tickles my nose and throat but I can see the men enjoying the strong cigars, they ain't for the young that's for sure, coffee finished I am pleased when Wade asks me if he would show me where to put up Ten-Ten he has come a far ways needs a breather. I jump at the chance and go to fetch Ten-Ten but Wade calls me to stop and tells me his horse has been trained as a war horse and he will not let strangers near him until I give them a proper introduction, he is a bit stuck up for a horse. Standing and removing his hat once more he thanks Ma for the snack and coffee and is very looking forward to a home cooked meal been some time since he had one, Ma in mock anger tells him he is just another Irish Rogue and sweet talker, Wade and I laugh as we walk over to Ten-Ten. Wade gives a small whistle and I stand with mouth open as I watch this amazing horse untie the knot with his teeth and walks over to meet Wade then puts his big head on his shoulder I can see clearly the bond between man and horse, "Ten-Ten this here is Nat he is a friend and you can trust him now do not be a snob and come say hi." The big horse puts his white velvety nose close to me and smells me to my pleasure he is calm, Wade said it is ok to pat him on the neck and talk to him a bit, I have to reach up to the big horses neck I am average for my size but I am only 12, the beautiful horse then nuzzles me and Wade says the horse has accepted me as a friend and will remember you so it is ok now to approach him. I lead the way to our small barn as we walk I ask Wade how he came to name his horse Ten-Ten, Wade gives off a bit of a chuckle and tells me that is a damn fine question he tells me never be afraid to ask if I do not know that is how we learn along with mistakes. "Nat the truth is I won him in a poker game off Luke Short in San Francisco with a pair of tens, Luke takes his losses well but loosing old Ten-Ten stung him some, but they come no better I figure and we are still Amigos."

Wade leads his horse to a stall and begins unsaddling him after all the gear is removed he takes a burlap cloth and wipes the horses back then finding a horse brush gives him a good brushing I go out back and gather up a big arm full of fresh cut hay and clover, then filled the water buck with fresh water, satisfied Wade grabs the Winchester and saddlebags and we head back to the house my stomach growls as I smell Ma cooking.

Just before supper our lone ranch hand the only man to stick with Pa riders in and stables his horse then makes his way to the house knocking what dust off he can with his old sombrero we are still outside waiting to be called in to eat, Pa may run the ranch but Ma runs the house and that ain't up for debate. Latigo Ryan is a big rough looking man with long grey hair and big moustache now nearing 60 he is a bit stooped and very much bow legged he and Jason Flynn cut a wide swathe when they young and half wild, as he nears the house he makes sure to spit out his chaw Ma does not like it one bit. Jason introduces the 2 men, Latigo raises an eyebrow, "Howdy Wade pleased to meet you, that is one hell of a horse you have there seems like we crossed paths before but I can't place it well folks call me Latigo due to my gentle nature, you are in treat Cara is the best dang cook in Territory, are you signing on ?" Pa tells his old friend they would be discussing it after supper best to talk on a full belly and sipping evening coffee, Ma calls to come and get it or she is throwing it out.

Latigo ain't fooling when he says Ma is a fine cook seems now company arrives around supper time, tonight it was big fried ham steaks with spuds, corn and fresh butter. It is no accident Pa built the house here for at the back there is a small cave like structure that acts like a root cellar and is cool all year long, Ma brings me some cold buttermilk Wade seeing it asks Ma for a glass he always did enjoy a cold glass of buttermilk, desert is my favorite fresh apple pie. When the meal is finished all the men heap compliments on Ma for a fine meal now the men head outside with their coffee and sit lighting up there smoke of choice Latigo likes his pipe in the evenings. Pa tells me to come and join them but to sit and listen, a closed mouth opens the mind. Pa breaks the calm of the evening, "Wade I recon you are a man that has crossed many rivers and been around some so you know I am shorthanded and I ain't going to sugar coat it they ran off scared their tales between their legs because Cecil Edwards who ones the bank. His is the Hanging C spread next to ours and aims to have it for his own does not seem to matter to him we were here first and it is filed land. "The hell of it is some prospector found what they call Fire opal in the hills just to the west there, seems this Opal rock is expensive but they need to come on my land to get it and I will have none of it, they do not care for the land, animals or its inhabitants he will rip it apart just to get some damn shiny rocks. "About a month ago one of the young hands was shot from ambush even Latigo lately has been dodging hot lead, Cecil is a man used to getting what he wants and has the man power he owns law so you can see what we are up against if you are smart you will be riding out after breakfast."

I watch Wade closely and find myself holding my breath waiting for his answer then he gives Pa one of his rare smiles, "Boss I will be riding out in the morning but only as far as Las Cruces I need a few supplies and send a couple telegrams if it is ok I will take the buckboard into town, when I get back you got yourself a hand, and I recon we together can get er done." Pa jumps up and quickly shakes Wades hand before he can change his mind and welcomes him the to the Double F connected, Latigo says to Wade when ready he will show him where to store his gear and where he can bunk. Looks like we got us a need hand, hot damn.

CHAPTER 2

MAKING ENEMIES

Early morning finds Wade driving the buckboard over a rough trail and heading towards the town of Las Cruces the drive is a good way to organize his thoughts and make a plan of action for when he gets to town, besides the telegrams and supplies he plans on visiting a few saloons not for drinking but saloons are the best way to gather information. Men get to blabbing especially after knocking back a few, amazing what you can learn just sitting quiet and sipping a beer. Wade looks around casually as he drives down the main street, it is a fair sized town with over 900 people its Spanish influence providing beautiful churches and a shaded plaza with a big fountain, he can smell the strong spices of Mexican cooking. He passes the bank and a couple of saloons and the Town Marshals office before he pulls up in front of Becks Emporium hitching the mare to the hitch rack he enters the store. A mild looking mature man in an apron is behind the counter and gives Wade a friendly welcome, after a few minutes of conversation Wade hands the store owner his list the asks where the telegraph office is, after getting directions he says he will be back shortly to pay and load up the wagon. The telegraph office is only a couple blocks so he decides to walk but grabs his Winchester rifle before leaving the store. Wade arrives at the telegraph building he tells the operator he needs to send 2 telegrams the operator says nothing but hands him 2 sheets of blank paper to write his messages his first message is to his old saddle partner Red Calhoun who last he heard was in Santa Fe, the message is short- RED IF NOT BUSY COME TO FLYNN RANCH LAS CRUCES BRING GUNS- WADE, the second was also to Santa Fe to a high ranking attorney by the name of Anson Franklin and requested he come to Las Cruces if able. Wade waits for the operator to send both messages satisfied he goes back to the Emporium to load his supplies when arrives back at the store he finds 2 big bruiser thug types standing by the front door he smiles to himself for it is an old game to him.

Taking a tighter grip on his rifle he walks up to the door and tries to enter, the 2 thugs stand shoulder to shoulder blocking his way smug and smiling, Wade takes a step back his green eyes flashing then like an adder he strikes he hits the man on his left with the butt of his rifle in the stomach the big mans breath explodes from him he then strikes the other brute across the ear with the unforgiving metal rifle barrel, shifting his feet Wade butt strokes the first man who drops like a stone, the fight ends when Wade smashes in his second opponents nose with the rifle butt. Calmly he steps over the fallen men and returns to the counter, Mr. Beck stands stunned by the sudden violence recovering he tells Wade he has everything ready, before he leaves the store he buys a 12 gauge greener shotgun 4 boxes of buckshot and 4 boxes of 44.40 cartridges they then load the wagon stepping over the bleeding and moaning men, thanking the storekeeper he turn the mare and drives the wagon to the first saloon the Prairie Lilly. Once again before entering the saloon he grabs up the Winchester after ordering a beer he finds an open table that puts his back to the wall after he lights up one of his black cigars he settles back and listens to the many conversations going on, then looking across the saloon he sees a large hard looking man dressed in fine buckskins looking back at him a Arkansas Toothpick stuck in the table in front of him sending the message he did not want company.

Grabbing his beer Wade walks over to the mountain mans table smiling down at the big man he asks, "Mr. Tobin it would be my pleasure to buy you a drink and have a few minutes of your time, I recon you know who I am but for know I go by the name Wade and rather people not knowing who I am for the present." Muskrat Tobin pulls the vicious looking blade from the table and using it points to a chair indicating Wade is welcome to join him, "Pleased to see you are still above the flowers Muskrat how has the trail be keeping you if you have nothing going on might have some rough fun for you and could get right ugly and dangerous?" Muskrat Bill Tobin is part of the Blue Hills Clan and does not care for people much with the exception of good honest hard fighting men like the one sitting across from him and knew him to be the Traveller. Peter and Paul Hennessy his Cousins speak highly of him after the big battle of Montana with United States Marshal Sudden Steele. Before a smiling Muskrat can answer the bat wing doors bang open and a sour looking Marshal by the name of Lee Gunner Brody enters, Gunner figures himself a real hellfire pistolero now having survived 2 stand up gun fights, he looks around then spotting Wade beelines it directly to where Bill and Wade sit. Muskrat is still holding the big knife and makes sure the Marshal sees it, Wade just moves the Winchester to a better angle for a quick grab and shot arriving at the table he ignores and focuses on Wade, "Stranger you made a big mistake in roughing up Cecil Edwards men he will have your hide nailed to the barn for it now I am placing you under arrest for assault and bodily harm, are you coming peaceful?"

Wade smiles to himself the game continues, "Why no Marshal cause I am not coming at all those men were deliberately blocking my way I just moved them a might now Marshal open your ears and keep your trap shut, I do not believe you were voted in or were the choice of the town council I recon old Cecil pays for that badge and the 2 bit gunman behind it". Brody face red moves his hand slowly to the .45 colt on his hip, "Marshal you touch that gun and I will kill you, now me and my friend are going to finish our beer and talk then I will be leaving town, be smart marshal go get yourself some pie and coffee." Gunner Brody is blind with rage but still sane enough to know this hard looking green eyed man will kill him not wanting to loose more face the Marshall tells Wade he better be out of town in half an hour or he is coming back, he leaves quicker than when he came in, Muskrat lets out a huge laugh, "Damn you got some big ones on you Amigo, that was damn fine to see now what is this shooting you were speaking of?"

Wade quickly tells Muskrat of the Flynn's troubles and he has hired on and sent for Red and a lawyer but he needs a man in the hills on the scout watching their backs or alert of any upcoming danger come in every 2nd day or so to report, cannot promise you much but maybe a fight a bullet in the guts but Cara Flynn is the best damn cook in the country that alone is worth fighting for," both men give of a quiet chuckle. "Wade lad you got yourself a scout I know the Flynn's to be good folks and that old mule headed Latigo and I go back more years than I care to remember you better get going you know Gunner will be back and not alone I will be out to the ranch tomorrow for war talk and supper." The men shake hands Wade goes right to the wagon and unties the mare without a backward glance he heads back to the barn.

CHAPTER 3

WATCHING BIG MEN WORK

The shadows are growing long when Wade arrives back at the Flynn ranch I have been watching for him a bit worried, he smiles at me as he pulls the buckboard up in front of the house and tells me to get busy unloading I am surprised and curious about the amount of supplies he brings back but I say nothing. Soon the supplies for the house are in and he then drops the remainder in the bunkhouse before unhitching the mare and giving her a bait of corn. Ma and Pa are also surprised and Pa just out and asks him why so much, "Well Jason I figure until the fight is over it is better to stay away from town and I doubt if the storekeeper will sell to us any longer, if it turns into a siege we have enough between the crops and supplies to last a long while better most of the stuff is for Ma, coffee, sugar, flour and the such, more ammunition and an extra shotgun for the house. "Well I do believe I might have poked the beast a bit but also got another good man to help us out but all that for after supper I am so dang hungry my stomach thinks my throats been cut, it has been a very interesting day."

After another one of Ma's delicious suppers Wade asks me if I would go to the bunkhouse and fetch his saddlebags, I am off like a shot and back within minutes, now what is this quiet man up to? The first thing he takes out is a paper bag filled with tobacco bark should keep the old Latigo in chaw for a spell, next he hands Pa another bag this one filled with black Mexican cigars now with that impish grin he hands be a paper bag looking inside I see it is filled with cherry sticks and licorice whips, last he hands man a wrapped brown package, opening she finds to her great delight finds it to be some emerald green cloth perfect making curtains and giving the house more colour. Wade in his usual manner waves of the thanks almost embarrassed then he tells us of the trip to town, "Well first off we got lucky I ran into Muskrat Tobin the old scout is going to join our cause and will be mostly out in the hills making sure we don't get any unwelcome surprises, he tells me him and Latigo here were hard riders and hell raisers together in the old days, I for one am happy to have him no better man in the wilds well maybe his cousins Peter and Paul. "Had a talk with the Marshal I recon it will be over smoking guns next time we cross paths, there is no help there as I figured he is bought and payed for, with my second telegram I sent a message to a friend of mine Anson Franklin in Sant Fe works directly for the Governor and deals mostly with land claims and government lands issues a damn fine lawyer and a good man to stand beside in a gun battle cold steel nerve."

"Jason this your ranch and you call the shots but I have been down this deadly trail a time or two and if you care to listen I got a few thoughts on how we may survive this but I believe before this is over it is going to get brutal and bloody, well boss there you have it your thoughts Hefe." I look to Pa his face etched in deep concentration Wade reaches over on puts his big hand in my paper candy bag pulls out a licorice whip and with a smile and wink begins eating the candy, somehow this made me feel less a child and part of the gathered group. Pa tells Wade he would like to hear what Wade, Latigo and Ma had to say then he would make his decision and Wade should get the ball rolling. "Boss my thought is if we can hang on until Lawyer Franklin can work this out and get some real law here first I recon we should fortify the ranch yard set up fighting positions with cover to retreat the house is the last line of defence. Then we lay in plenty of wood and water the cold cellar gives us the edge to hold of a long attack, Nat tomorrow you and I are going to water the roof, fire is always the weapon of desperate brutal enemies. "Starting tomorrow morning no one rides alone for any reason, Cara you and Nat I would be much obliged if you stuck close to the house, just not for your safety but you get the shutters and doors covered and secure quick if put upon. Muskrat will be here tomorrow and with luck old hard head Red should be here in a days those 2 madcaps are worth 20 of theirs, now one last thing we will have to start keeping watch at night, I don't think the land grabbers are prepared yet but just in case old Ten Ten and I will be keeping an eye on things, that old horse of mine has a bit of wild in him and better than any watchdog, so that's my piece, Latigo Amigo lets get your thoughts."

The old cowboy knows the score he has fought in 2 range wars and survived and being a man of good common sense knew what Wade said to be true he just told Pa if he were smart he would latch on to Wades ideas. Ma had little to say but in her matter of fact tone stated when the fight comes she will be ready no son of a bitch is taking her families home, Pa smiles so proud of her, a true western woman hard as iron soft as goose feathers those that don't know will find out my Ma is one tough customer. Pa like his old Pard Latigo knows sense when he hears it and agrees with Wades ideas the only thing he added as of tomorrow we will rotate the guard, Wade asks me to fetch Ten Ten and just put a short rope on his neck and tell him he is going on watch he will come gentle. I dash off to the barn, I do as Wade asks and within a couple minutes the big horse is following me back to the house like a trained dog. Wade is waiting Winchester in hand the group are off doing last minute duties before it gets to dark, "Thanks Nat looks like you got yourself a friend and old Ten Ten is right particular on who he will tolerate, damn uppity horse, I talked with your Pa and if you like you can come out and sit watch with me a bit before hitting the hay, so you up for some scouting work Hoss?"

Ma has raised no dimwits I readily accept excited to have some time with the quiet fighter and now friend, he gives me a leg up and I sit bareback atop Ten Ten Wade starts walking and the beautiful horse follows soon Wade finds a spot on a small rise with a few tall thin trees and decides this is a good spot to keep watch, he then tells me to climb off and we will find a comfortable spot. We now sit with our backs to the trees it will be dark in a few minutes Wade puts his long gun beside him but in reach for a quick grab and begins my education. "Nat lad I recon it is a good time to give you a few pointers on doing night sentry duty, knowledge is always wasted if not passed on, now before it getting dark you look over the country in front real close take note of things like that pile of rocks just yonder and that patch of bush memorize the area because at night everything looks different your eyes can play tricks on you." "Now another thing never look directly at anything sweep with your eyes to be a good guard you must remain quiet and still, if there is an enemy out there he is looking for the same things, never look into light or fire when night scouting you will lose your night vision for near 20 minutes plenty of time to get dead, and use senses, it is a fact an Indian sneaking up on you can smell you therefore find and kill you. Remember your job is to protect and warn others of danger if you fail, they may all be killed, now take a good look at the country and tell me what landmarks you see."

It is full dark now Wade sits quiet I can hear Ten Ten munching on grass and the chirping of crickets in a quiet voice Wade tells me always listen for the night sounds like the crickets and frogs if things go real quiet good chance trouble is near, I look into the darkness damn things are scary at night but as my eyes adjust I am amazed by how much I can see but it still looks like things are moving out there gives me the creeps but I say nothing. I spend about an hour with the nighthawk before he sends back to the house time to get some rest before I good he tells me a good soldier always rests and eats when he can may be a long spell until you get either again, rest keep the brain sharp. I thank Wade and give old Ten Ten some attention then head back to the house and my bed, I wonder just who Wade is I am old enough to know he is no 40 dollar a month cowhand, a mystery man for sure.

When I come down to breakfast everyone is at the table I quickly give my good mornings and tear into one of Ma's big breakfasts, she says a man needs a big breakfast to hold him though his work day, I glance through the kitchen window and see a rider coming in slow and steady I call to the men someone is coming. Wade says should be old Pax Hennessey coming in for breakfast the men grab their coffees and rifles and go outside to wait on the lone rider. The rider draws near enough to see his features I ain't sure who this is but it ain't Mr. Tobin this man about the same height as Wade but a good 20 pounds heavier under his big grey sombrero was a long mane of bright red hair and shaded bright blue eyes, his skin a bit red from sunburn but the thing that really caught my eye he is wearing a two gun rig with 2 bone handled .45 colt peacemakers in it holsters, like Wade he rode a fine horse a big Buckskin gelding with beautiful long black mane and tail. He pulls up in front of our small, group and gives a off a big honest smile, Wade looks at the man in a bit of disbelief," Howdy Red you old sheep rustler damn good to see you Pard but how did you get here so quick, these folks here are Jason and Cara Flynn it is their ranch and this Buckaroo is Nat a top hand and I recon you remember Latigo, folks this hombre is the man I sent for Red Calhoun climb on down and sit to coffee."

Red says that is the best offer he heard all day, Ma hurries into the house and brings our new visitor a coffee after cigars are passed around and lit Red gives the story of his fast arrival, "I will tell you what new of some folks travels fast out here I am just out riding along minding my own business when I stop into a cantina to parch my thirst when I hear from the Mexican telegraph that there is a man named Wade down Las Cruces way stirring up trouble. "Well it not take much brains to figure it was you and knowing you I figured I best find you and as usual keep you from getting all shot up, now how about telling me just what in tarnation is going on here."

CHAPTER 4

THE ENEMY STRIKES

The banker and ranch owner Cecil Edwards is sitting at his desk giving the Marshal a hard look unhappy how things went with the stranger working for Flynn now, he did not like mystery he worked with facts, Cecil is a fat man in an expensive store bought suit and a bad attitude, there is no humor at all in the man, greed is his mistress and evil is his partner, nothing or no one mattered to him but cold hard cash and the money from the opal mine could make him a millionaire, he almost smiles. Sitting across the desk from him is Marshal Gunner Brody and hired gunman and assassin Blaze Conrad, Blaze is well known throughout the south for being ruthless and bloody he always travels with 6 hardcase gunmen are pure bad medicine, without a doubt a tough crew, Cecil also has 10 men on fighting wages and a dozen or more tough old cowhands more than enough to take out Jason Flynn and that damn Stanger who has sided with him. Scowling he looks across at his hired gunmen," That damn stranger has sent a wire to a lawyer in the Capital this means we have to get Flynn off the land and time has run out we are now near the end game, no more kit gloves Blaze tonight you and your men are going gather up a few good men and supplies and you are going to get them in good position for defence we will invoke squatters rights. "Gunner you ride to my ranch get Slim Tanner and 6 of the hired guns I am dearly paying for and you attack the ranch this way we have them pinned down while we get men on that mine and if you kill a few while you are at it all the better, now coordinate your attacks for lets say tonight at 9 the darkness should work to our advantage, now you over paid gun throwers get the hell out my office and next time we meet there better be good news."

Suppertime once again finds me sitting beside my new best friend Wade, there is something about this quiet man that makes me feel comfortable and safe, at first glance Wade looks quite tame but once you look into those blazing green eyes you know that this man is iron on iron hard and does not need to prove it. His friend Red is almost Wades opposite always funning and joking with a big smile but like Wade he is wang leather tough and according to Latigo Red is a magician with his Winchester one of the best rifle shots in the country and is greased lightning with his heavy hitting Schofield .45s. I am startled by a knock on the door the men instinctively reach for their sidearms, "Open up it is Muskrat hope there is still coffee on, we are going to need it," I go to the door and look up at the mountain of a mountain man I am a bit frightened he looks fearsome with his face scars and braided hair, but then he smiles and pats me tenderly on the shoulder, "Howdy there Hoss I am Muskrat pleased to meet you do you think you could fetch me a coffee it is time for some war talk." Introductions are made all around coffee is poured and old Muskrat starts telling us of what he expects for upcoming trouble and it is going to happen real soon as in tonight, seems the sly old mountain man was listening at the open window in Cecil's office and overheard their plans for the 2 attacks coming this evening, so he reconed he better high tail it out here and warn us, looks like we got a scrap like it or not.

Wade sits back in his chair and lights up a thin black cigar his face void of expression but like Pa says a duck on water all calm on top but legs going like mad under water, then sitting forward begins to lay out his plans to spoil the black riders night, "Well as I see it we cannot let these villians get a foothold on the mine site so Muskrat if he is up for some fun and myself will handle the men at the mine the rest of you will protect the ranch I suggest Red be in charge of the reception I noticed from the barn you could get a deadly cross fire going but I leave it to you, I am taking Muskrat because he does his best fighting in the open Apache style, should give them fellas a right warm reception." Now we better get er in gear we ain't got much time Nat while I get my gear together could you go throw the saddle on old Ten Ten be much appreciated." I am off in a flash old Ten Ten and I are becoming fast friends but now I slow down and take my time getting the horse ready I want to show Wade I am up to the task, the men are waiting when I lead the big horse back to the house, Wade is armed and loaded for bear, besides his 2 pistols he has a .56 calibre 5 shot revolving rifle fine weapon has the repeating action of a pistol and the accuracy of a rifle and slung over his back is a sawed off double barrelled greener. His clothing is now different he wears moccasins instead of boots and has on a longer black duster coat Muskrat did not need to change he never wears anything but buckskins he is standing beside his huge blue nosed mule Knothead waiting patiently but obvious he wants to hit the trail. Wade thanks me and climbs into the hurricane deck of Ten Ten, ready to go Muskrat looks to his riding partner, "Well Traveller my old friend let's go pick us a fight, "with that they turn and ride away I stand there with my mouth open, hot damn Wade is the Traveller them outlaws are sure in for it now, they got themselves a ring tailed tiger by the tail.

I watch until I can no longer see the riders then I hear Red calling everyone together to begin preparing for our unwelcome visitors, first thing is he sends me to get extra wood from the pile we do not know how long we would be under attack, water is no problem we have a reservoir of cold fresh water, the house is built from stone so bullets will do no harm. Red says he and Latigo will be in the barn and if lucky we should catch them flat footed, but no one is to fire until he does then cut loose. Red then goes and pulls off the gun rack our single shot 12 gauge shotgun and puts a big shell in the tube snapping it shut he hands it to me with a couple extra shells and tells me my job is the back door if anyone tries to break in point and shoot right trough the door, and I must not hesitate Red tells me with a smile. "Shoot first and let God sort them out." Pa has his .45 colt tucked into his belt and his Henry rifle in hand, Ma has her Spencer and is a real fine shot with it often putting venison and turkey on the table, we then put the shutters up on all the windows and once Red and Latigo head to the barn we bar the door. This is the first time I learn waiting is harder than doing I am as edgy as a wet cat, Pa talks in his soft way telling me we got us a tough crew and the Banker will have less fighting men come morning. Just then we hear Red call out they are coming and to get ready I lay on my stomach the shotgun tucked into my shoulder my eyes locked on the back door, no SOB is coming through-sure as shooting.

Traveller and Muskrat arrive at the mine just as a huge golden sun is setting in the western hills, knowing they do not have much time to get ready it will be dark soon, the horses are left at the base of the hill sheltered by high rock ridges, both men grab their weapons extra ammo and supplies and begin a quick search for a good ambush spot above the intruders with some cover. Muskrat finds a good spot and the men move in to prepare leaving his rifle Traveller grabs the sack he brought along and walks out about 20 yards and places 2 pumpkin sized rocks along side each other but about 12 feet apart then pours the contents evenly over both rocks emptying the sack, nodding his satisfaction he heads back, muskrat greets him with a huge smile.

Blaze can now see the large hill where the Flynn mine is to be he smiles once he gets men on top 2 men with rifles can hold off an army for days, following the mercenary are 9 hard and desperate men everyone meaner than a grizzly with a sore paw, Blaze looks back at his men he has already given them orders anyone on the hill is to be killed shot down like a rabid dog, no witnesses. Gunner, Slim and 6 hired guns are now approaching the ranch in full darkness it is near time to attack, Gunner is not sure on his best plan of attack should they go in blasting and lay siege from cover or sneak in close real quiet and cut loose, being a man of little imagination or patience he decides they will hit the ranch house hard and fast, but tells 2 men to go round back hit them from 2 sides, he tells the boys to get ready they are going to be riding in hell for leather. The hour of the joint attacks is near both outlaw gangs get ready for their joint assaults, a killing lust begins to envelope the attackers the desire to kill so intense it borders madness.

Blaze might be a first rate gun thrower but he was not a man of the wilds he and his men thinking themselves moving quiet were loud as a brass band to the waiting men, Muskrat whispers to Wade that them fools would be dead right quick in Pache country. One thing outdoor men know is sound travels far at night Traveller smiles and snugs the butt of his rifle into his shoulder and waits soon dark figures can be seen approaching they are now almost to the 2 big rocks Wade set out. Aiming carefully now Traveller fires at the rock on the left then the right, the night turns into day as the piles of gunpower flare leaving the outlaws totally stunned and exposed. Muskrat opens up with his big .50 and a man screams Traveller drops 2 more outlaws before darkness falls, both men then draw their six guns and spray the area in from of them hot lead fills the air, the sounds of men running away yelling in fear and anger are heard now the attack and occupation of the mine is a horrible failure for Blazer. When the gunslinger gets back the horses only 5 men are waiting and 2 are wounded, he wonders why the side of his face is sticky putting his hand to his ear he jumps with pain as he realizes the lower half of his right ear is missing his hand comes away covered in blood, Blazer for the first time in his life feels fear, fear of the quiet stranger.

The thunder of hooves and the barking of guns fill the night as Gunner and his men slam into the ranch yard, Red and Latigo are both masters of the long gun and within a few heartbeats 2 men lay dead in the yard and 2 wounded men are riding like Satan is on their tails away from the killing zone. I listen to the gunfire but keep my eye on the back door as Traveller told me I see the handle lift I pull the trigger sending a big load of 12 gauge buckshot through the door, I hear a man yell in pain I break open the big gun and slam another shell in but I hold my fire I believe them polecats want no more of me and the big gun. Gunner and Slim make it away alive from the ranch as well as one of the men he sent around back, Gunner has been shot in the fleshy part just above his left hip the bullet goes clean through another bullet has ripped his right cheek open the sickening white of his check bone can be seen even in the dark. Slim is hurting bad a rifle bullet has smashed his left knee it is a gory mess of blood and bone, the last remaining outlaw got off somewhat lucky but will be awhile until he gets all the wood slivers out of his face.

My eyes sting from the acid smoke of the guns and my ears ring for some unknown the sudden quiet makes me nervous, I walk over and place the shotgun on the counter, then Red calls out all clear and they are coming back to the house Pa takes the bar off the front door and opens it fresh air starts to fill the room. I watch Red and Latigo check that the men laying in the yard their 6 guns ready and cock in case one is playing possum. Satisfied Red returns his hogleg to its holster, the battles of the opal mine and Flynn ranch are over the enemy has taken its lumps and will have to lick its wounds hopefully the law will get here before they have another go at us.

CHAPTER 5

DEADLY FIRE

Traveller and Muskrat get back just as the morning birds wake in song the sky now gray I tried to stay awake until the men got back from the mine but fail and wake to voices talking in the kitchen and the delicious smells of coffee and fried bacon, rubbing the sleep from my eyes I join the men at the table. All look a bit wore out but relaxed and relieved everyone on the ranch survived a deadly hard fought night. Ma pours me half a cup of coffee I sweeten it up with 4 spoonfuls of sugar and blow on the steaming hot brew waiting for it to cool, Ma needlessly apologizes that it will only be biscuits and bacon for breakfast. To a man they tell Ma how they appreciate her cooking for them and she has been spoiling them to getting where they are getting stretched out in the middle. It is a beautiful sunny morning with a sweet touch of cool and a slight breeze, Pa tells me I am to go feed the stock while he and the other men bury the dead outlaws, Wade backs up Pa saying it is better the old hands take care of this grim work, well I ain't fighting Pa and the Traveller over it and secretly I am relieved and tell Pa I will get to it right away.

I watch from the barn as Latigo ropes and ties the legs of the dead then wrapping the rope around his saddle horn he then one at a time drags the men away from the ranch yard to a spot just off the rutted trail where digging will be easy there will only be one grave holding the remains of 3 evil men and the country is much better for it. Red has the forge heated up and is burning something into a large flat piece of wood, just as Wade and Pa are done throwing dirt on the dead men's faces when Red emerges from the shed and calls to me come along with him to the gravesite together we walk over to the mass grave I can see now Red made a grave marker by burning the words into the wood with a red hot running iron. Red takes one of the shovels and hammers the wooden marker deep into the ground at the head of the grave he then stands back smiling and admiring his handiwork near the top of the marker he burnt in 3 crosses to show the number of dead men beneath the crosses he carved the following words, "THEY CAME IN THE NIGHT EVIL IN THEIR HEARTS DIED SUDDENLY OF LEAD POISONING NOW REFORMED." Damn that Red is a character the sign gets a hard chuckle from the men, it is a tough land with tough men, I look up and see a rider coming not sparing the spurs dust flying behind his horses thundering hooves I watch as Pa and the men strap on their guns always wary and ready for trouble.

The rider is Southpaw Felix a friend of Muskrat's he slows up before reaching us so not to cover us with dust dismounting he shakes hands with his old friend and then tells Wade he has a telegraph from the capitol for him figured he would want to see it right quick so he rode hell for leather to get here. The men thank Southpaw Pa tells me to go ask Ma to put the coffee on they will have coffee and smokes on the wooden benches outside and see what the telegram says, I am not sure why but I am anxious and excited I never even seen one before got to be real important. Southpaw and the other men stand and remove their hats when Ma brings out the huge coffee pot and tin mugs returning to the house she retrieves a big platter of fresh baked cookies, you would think old South had died and gone to heaven after thanking Ma tears into them with a vengeance. The Traveller opens the telegram and reads it out loud to the coffee group, it is from his friend and lawyer Anson Franklin, "WADE -GOVERNOR AWARE OF SITUATION IS SENDING JUDGE ELLIOT- UNITED STATES MARSHAL WAYNE- AND MYSELF TO INVESTIGATE ARRIVING 16TH THIS MONTH-ANSON FRANKLIN ATTORNY." I go over to the wall and check the calendar that is the day after tomorrow good the sooner the better Pa and Wade talk it over and decide there is no danger to the ranch so the whole kit and kaboddle will be going into town. I am excited I have not been off the ranch in what seems forever, and I figure no matter what happens it ought be a right interesting day.

The next 2 days pass quickly I spend most of my time with Wade and Red, with big men it is best to listen close and ask questions both men have a way of teaching as they talk and a person can learn a lot if they take the time to listen. I watch the Traveller he moves like a cat no wasted moves quiet, smooth and he is deceptively strong and quick, rattlesnake strike reflexes. The Travellers quiet manner makes it hard for me to accept him to be the killer people make him out to be. Red tells me the Traveller never shot anyone that did not deserve it and they all took hot lead in the front in stand-up fights, and there is no brag Red has seen the Travellers graveyards, Wade also has little patience with bullies and thieves the smart ones cross the street when they see him coming. The night before we go to town Ma whipped up one hell of a good supper with roast beef, potatoes, gravy and corn, for dessert a huge dried apple pie, I eat until I durn near burst, the men just gush over Ma's meal. Wade tells Ma he and I will take care of the dishes and cleaning up the kitchen, Ma of course politely tries to refuse the offer but when the Traveller digs his spurs in, be easier moving a mountain, it is a fine night one of the meals you remember your whole life.

Finally the day comes to head into town, Southpaw and Muskrat left well before morning light they wanted to check the hills and mine then they will meet us in time for the stage, Pa and Ma will take the buckboard the rest of the men will ride. Wade leads Ten

Ten out of the barn but also brings one of our gelded mustangs named Penny for the copper colour of his hair Wade tells me I will ride in with the rest of the men. I am sure if I had a buttoned vest, I would have popped them buttons clean off with the pride I feel riding with the big men. Wade and the rest of the outriders are not trusting men all had their long guns out and watch the skyline all the way into town only sheathing their rifles when the buckboard turns onto main street. Pa pulls up in front of the general store the stage depot is right across the street we are a bit early the stage ain't due for another 30 or so minutes western time does not work real well with clocks. Red escorts Ma into the store, wisely no one tries stopping them unlike Wade Red would shoot them dead and not blink an eye, the rest of us cross the street to the stage depot Southpaw is already there but no sign of Muskrat, pipes and cigars are lit and the talk is quiet,. Red comes from the store and joins us he hands me a cherry sasparilla and tells the group the storekeeper is being real pleasant and polite to Ma, everyone now knows Banker Edwards is finished. The soda pop is delicious I take another big swig and watch as Muskrat comes hurrying towards us by his expression I can tell it is trouble of some sort, Wade hands the old mountain man a cigar and tells him to catch his breath and tell us what has him so agitated.

"Traveller that gun thrower Blaze is calling you out and swears to gut shoot you right here on main street he has had just enough rot gut to make him mean, and he is real displeased with you for shooting his ear off. He says to meet him here after the stage comes in so your friends can watch you die, if you don't show he will hunt you and shoot on sight, now Wade I seen him haul iron down San Antonio way and he is lightning quick and most hits what he aims at, and I mean John Wesley Hardin good, you will have to be hard today Hoss." Wade is quiet you would think he was being told of a church supper or the price of corn, in a low serious tone he asks Muskrat to return to the saloon and tell the would be bad man I will gladly accept his challenge all he needs do is step into the middle of the street that is if he has the guts. Muskrat happily agrees and tells Southpaw to come along they were going to check the town and rooftops to make sure it is a fair duel, Wade shakes hands just in case and thanks the men before they leave.

Shortly after the mountain men leave the noise of the stage arriving can be heard the driver Whip Spinner brings the stage to an abrupt halt cursing the horses dust fills the air, old Whip thinks this great fun, the stagecoach door opens and 3 men looking worse for wear gladly exit the 2 groups meet and introductions are made all along. I'll tell you what that Marshal Wayne is one big tough looking character, damn glad he is on our side, the Judge is a short roundish manner but no nonsense about him he commanded respect for his position he tells the group they will first go over to the bank and deal with Edwards there is enough evidence to put him in State prison for a good 5 or more years. Just then Blazer steps into the middle of the street, Red tells the new arrivals about the challenge and upcoming gun battle, all the men are western and know the Traveller has no choice, not to fight would brand him a coward is worse than being dead. Wade pulls the .44 Russian revolver from its holster and gives it one last look see before returning it. He shakes hands all around including mine and gives me a smile and wink then tells me to get my ass off the street bullets do not care who they kill.

After taking a deep breath the Traveller steps into the street and faces the hired killer, he then begins his WALKDOWN approaching Blaze in long quick strides I find myself holding my breath watching the drama of death unfold, not a sound is heard Wade keeps closing in. Blazer blinks and with lightning speed reaches for his smokewagon the .45 colt comes out fast and sure the barrel coming in line with Travellers chest, before he can pull the trigger 2 big.44 lead slugs smash into Blazer it feels he has been hit by a meat axe, chest bones are shattered and are driven through the already dead mans heart and lungs the .45 slips from a dead hand. Before he falls Traveller takes careful aim and puts a chuck of hot lead through Blazers skull, the hot lead shedding and searing brain matter, 6 inches of skull are blown off the back of his head red mist fills the air, always make sure your enemy is dead.

The Traveller always finishes his man with a head shot, a man may survive bullets to the body Cole Younger was shot 11 times and survived but a head shot is permanent that way he knows men that should be dead are not on his backtrail. Damn that was quick half a heartbeat and a man lies dead the thought frightens me, I learned a lot this day, Gunner and what was left of his men were seen riding hell for leather south to Texas, the Banker got 4 years in the state pen and did not live to get out. Wade and Red hung around helping Pa get things back in order and then gathered a honest foreman and mining crew to work the mine. Grown now and a man of wealth and influence I spend my time travelling and working to make the State a safe place to live, but to this day I remember the lessons well taught to me by the quiet gunfighter and try my best to live by the Code

A DECENT COWBOY DOES NOT TAKE WHAT BELONGS TO SOMEONE ELSE AND IF HE DOES HE DESERVES TO BE STRUNG UP AND LEFT FOR THE FLIES AND COYOTES- JUDGE ROY BEAN

STORY 6

WHEN YOU MAKE A PROMISE KEEP IT

CHAPTER 1

THE PROMISE

Sgt. Duff Fleming formally a Scottish born soldier of fortune now rides the edge of the mountain country near Grand Cache Alberta which looks over the Smoky river, he is following a blood tail and footprints of a someone bad hurt but trying to cover his sign. This puzzles the Sgt, he knows it is his duty to find this person for he now wears the scarlet tunic of the North West Mounted police, and it is duty above all. The Mountie can tell by the staggering tracks the man must be near the end he would find him soon and hopefully still alive, it is only minutes when he sees an old man who appears to be a trapper sitting with his back to a tree, at hearing the Sgt's horse he gamely tries to bring his rifle up for a shot, he sees the red tunic and lets the weapon slip from his fingers. Duff Fleming grabs his canteen and rushes over to the sitting man, kneeling beside the trapper he quickly checks to see how bad the man is wounded he discovers 2 bullet wounds in the mans back high up. This old man is one tough cob most men would have curled up and died from the hot lead in their backs this man must have a strong reason for staying alive. At first glance the man is unconscious and his breathing is low and raspy, Duff figured he would just sit with the man passed over then her would bury him, suddenly the wounded man grabs tightly on to the Mounties tunic and with his blue eyes blazing begins to speak.

"Thank God its you them backshooting varmits are on my backtrail and intend to rob me of my life's earning, my name is Joe Dobson now I know I am dead meat but the money I have is for my Granddaughter Tracey Dobson she lives in Calgary, she is just barely 18 and in danger my son married bad into a vipers nest of uppity and greedy in laws. They will stop at nothing to get my baby girl's money even murder I recon the assholes who killed me were hired by them. "I know you Mounties to be men of your word and will hold to a promise I need you to promise to make sure Tracey get what is rightfully hers and no harm comes to her, they are all a bad bunch but the worst of them is her uncle and aunt Ben and Abby Weatherby, and she is the maybe the worst, evil wench. Mountie I ain't got much time the gold is in a belt around my stomach now promise me you will do it Mountie, promise me please." Sgt. Fleming looks down at the dying man he is filled with both anger and sadness putting his hand on the old trappers soldier, "Joe I am Duff Fleming of the clan Kirkcaldy and on my clans honour and banner swear that I will help wee Miss Tracey gets the gold and no harm will come to her even if it means my life, right and justice will prevail, rest now old man you earned it may Saint Peter have the gates open for you when you arrive do you want me to bury you?" The death rattle slows in Joes chest with his last remaining breaths he thanks Duff and says to leave him lie give himself back to the wilderness he loved then all goes quiet the old trapper has crossed over, the Sgt., puts 2 copper coins in the old mans dead hands to pay the ferryman at the river Styx.

Duff gently straightens out the old mans body and crosses the arms over chest, he then removes the heavy gold laden money belt and the old mans rifle, 6 gun and knife so they do not fall into the wrong hands, after taking one last look to make sure all was in order he climbs up on the big bay gelding and heads back to his outpost and telegraph office. He has to notify the Inspector of the murder and the Sgt's intentions if the boss allows it, Duff Fleming is now smiling and thinking to himself that the men who killed Joe come after him soon he will as the NWMP code says bring them in alive but the Sgt does not care he will be more than happy to send a couple dogs to hell at Joes feet, one way or another the bloody bastards will pay.

CHAPTER 2

DUFF FLEMING

Like most NWMP officers were from all over the Commonwealth and it is for Duff Fleming born and raised in Kirkcaldy Scotland a rough port town were he learned to fight and brawl, his is the Kirkcaldy clan a clan known for its bravery and word his ancestors reach back to the ancients. When of age Duff went to sea and still as a young man was first mate on a Dutch merchant ship, twice his ship was attacked but the raiders were repelled by the ferocity of Duff Fleming and his men. After a time Duff was taken from the sea and hired out as a mercenary fighting in Iraq, India and Afghanistan with each battle his name became known to the generals as a brave but smart fighter winning battles by outsmarting his enemies. He was becoming a very well paid senior officer he would probably still be fighting but he came across an article in a London paper of this new police organization in Canada recruiting men for police work in the wilds of the western lands. When Duff Fleming decides he calls them fast and walks away tough as soon as his contact expired with his current employer he grabbed his pay and began his journey to the colonies filled with outlaws, wild Indians and whiskey traders. Flynn loves riding in new country but he was ill prepared for the immense beauty of the foothills, valley's and the majestic heights of the snow top covered Rocky Mountains as with many a man Duff fell in love and became a man of the west.

How odd and different his job as a Police officer was compared to being a soldier for hire, for one thing him and 3 Constables police an area bigger than some countries he fought in, another instead of stealth and concealment his job now was to stand out in the revered red tunic to make his presence known and to inform people he was there representing the Queen across the big water. One policy Duff is not fond of which is strongly enforced by Inspector Steele is that a Mountie only draws his weapon if he is going to use it, but one thing sure if the outlaws see a Mountie reach for his rifle or pistol someone is going to get killed. Duff being no fool knew his best chance for survival and success is to find himself a experienced teacher to teach him the ways of the wild and the tracking skills of a plainsman with this he was very fortunate when fate introduced him to Mato which means bear a Dakota Sioux assigned as Scout for the Mounties. Mato is no longer young, streaks of gray are showing in his long black hair, he has a slight limp from a spear wound in the hip given to him by a Blackfoot warrior, he is tall for a native being near 6 ft and has a bit of a heavy build but can move smooth and quiet like a panther, despite his age Mato is still iron on iron hard and is a man best left be.

Duff and Mato soon became friends the Dakota likes to hear Duff's tales of far foreign places, battles and the exotic women and the Sgt is a good learner he listens and asks good questions in the short time together Mato considers Duff a skilled tracker and scout, out in the wilds you learn and adapt fast or die quick. Duff is hoping to enlist his fiend to make the hard dangerous ride for one the Sioux knew the country and the back trails better than anyone and if it comes to fighting Mato is skilled in many weapons and a good man to have on your side, lastly Mato enjoys any chance he can to kill white men and not hang for it. Duff is still a good days ride from his remote outpost and his instincts are screaming at him there are men following his back trail Duff knew these polecats would not hesitate to shoot him down and steal Miss Tracey's gold, he smiles to himself thinking of a story he heard in India on how a man was hunting a tiger and all went well until he caught it, tonight the killers will meet the big cat.

Daylight is now fading as the sun sets behind the immense western mountains Duff knows of a camp close by that he has used before good water, cover and a wide field of fire, he curses knowing he dare not make a fire and no fire means no coffee, for this a price must be paid taking a mans evening coffee from him is downright insulting. Arriving at the campsite Duff tends to his horse unsaddling and picketing him close to the water and thick green grass, he then fills his canteen and checks both his Winchester 44.40 level action rifle and the .450 Adams revolver satisfied he pulls some cold bannock and hard jerky from his saddlebags and calls it supper. Duff is still displeased of having to wash down his meager supper with water but shakes it off leaning his back against a tree trunk he settles in to catch a couple hours rest before he heads out on the night raid he suspects its going to be a long dangerous night. Time passes quickly before the Sgt leaves camp he exchanges his tunic and high top leather boots for Moccasins and buckskin shirt picking up the canteen and his long gun Duff heads back the way he came at a ground eating jog, his movements smooth no wasted energy, his eyes constantly searching the area for signs of a fire or a sulphur flaring to fire up a smoke. After a couple miles Duff slows to a brisk walk more of a march, from experience the Sgt begins to use his other senses for sound travels a long way over the dark land and even smoke from a quirly lingers in the air a long while.

Duff is just beginning to doubt himself about being hunted when out of the corner of his eye he sees the light of a fire in the distance and it is to big to be an Indian fire smiling again Sgt Fleming and once again moves off at a fast trot time for a wee chat with the unknown travellers. Laying prone behind a big clump of a wild rose bush about 20 yards from the camp Duff looks over the 4 men sitting around the fire at a glance the Mountie knows these men are a team of hired killers. Each of the men are dressed in identical long black duster coats and black hats, each and every one armed to the teeth and ready for bear, Duff smiles, killers yes but not western men no guard posted and all looking into the fire taking away their night vision. Duff crawls slowly to his left just beyond the campfires light to get in a better position to cover all 4 men, the Mountie takes a deep breath and stands rifle cocked and ready in a loud authoritative voice now announces his presence, "Hands up lads or the devil may take you I am Sgt Duff Fleming of the North West Mounted Police now no fast moves or it will be breakfast with Lucifer himself, now toss your weapons in a pile in front of you and I mean right bloody now."

Some people just don't listen the black rider to the far left makes a grab for his revolver in his shoulder holster Duff fires the Winchester from the hip the big chuck of hot lead smashes the mans breast bone driving large sliver of bone through the doomed mans heart and lungs he died quick, quickly Duff jacks a live round into the chamber, "Ok boyos anyone else like a try I got lots of lead left, now be good lads and do what your are told." This time the remaining 3 black riders moved slow and deliberate with no tricks the Mounties message is crystal clear do as he says or die, Duff does not move closer to the men but stays in the darkness appearing to the nervous men as some sort of Phantom, Duff now begins his interrogation.

"So mercenaries and hired killer is my guess men of the west you are not I am surprised your scalps are not on some Blackfoot warriors coup stick, no I am thinking you polecats are the ones who did old Joe the miner in and tried to rob him. You are scum to try to take the money rightfully belonging to his niece but the old man showed you what iron on iron hard means, I would arrest you men but I have more pressing business but before I leave you will tell me who hired you." The black rider in the middle had a nasty looking scar under his left eye running almost back to his ear seems he will talk for his men, "Sgt we have done nothing we are just travelling though the country on out way to Saskatchewan seems the Cree's are getting riled, we know nothing of any killing, you have no evidence or right to treat us badly." Sgt Fleming lets out a laugh then once again fires the Winchester the black riders leaders left ear vanishes in a red mist, "Wrong answer asshole now I will ask one last time and if I do not hear the truth you will lose your other ear you talk laddie or I will shoot you to doll rags, now talk," to emphasis his point he levers another big shell into the chamber. Tough looking men are often weak inside tough when in packs or have the upper hand but when facing danger alone is another thing the scarred rider has had enough and begins to spill his guts, "Ok you win Mountie I ain't saying we killed Joe but we were sent looking for him a gal hired us, nasty piece of work beautiful and totally ruthless cut her mothers throat for the gold in her teeth goes my the name Abby Weatherby married to Ben who is just as bad. They hired us to get the gold any way possible, now that's all I know Sgt and that the truth be obliged if you don't shoot me no more."

"Men who will kill an old man for his hard earned money and try to rob a young lady of what is rightfully hers are beneath contempt, bloody pond scum, now you the man on the right I want you to get up very slowly gather up all the rifles then move over to that big rock and smash them to pieces now move," the black rider wisely said nothing but did what he was told destroying all the long guns, "now go to the picket line and untie the horses, move slow now killing 1, 2 or all of you makes no difference to me." Once the horse are freed Duff fires 3 quick shots at the horses feet the terrified animals scatter quickly into the night, "I will be leaving you lads now you have your sidearms for safety and your will find your horses about 2 miles south a nice creek and good grass, now the important part we all know this is far from over but I now know your faces and when we meet again I will arrest you for murder or I will shoot you down like rabid skunks, might be time to look for other work." It took the black riders a few minutes to realize their deadly visitor is long gone, the scarred rider is filled with hatred at the Mountie no man treats him this way and lives, that Mountie is going to suffer plenty and beg for death before him and the boys are done working him over, plenty."

CHAPTER 3

BLOODY PLANS

Sgt Fleming reaches his remote outpost without further incident and quickly gets to work preparing for his ride and getting young Miss Tracey her inheritance, one of Mato's nephews Little Wolf helps around the outpost things like making sure there is plenty of firewood and water tending to the animals and a hundred other tasks, I send Little Wolf to find his Uncle and tell him to come quick and bring his guns. All the Mountie outposts have telegraphs sits and writes out as briefly as possible the situation and asks permission from Inspector Steele to keep his promise to the old miner and get the gold safely to Miss Tracey.

Abby Weatherby is worried and angry there should have been word by now from Drew Hanson the leader of the infamous band of hired killers known as the Black Law, how hard is it to find and kill one old man, she knows if that gold gets to her niece Tracey her dreams of becoming a member of high society shattered, her anger mounts. Abby at first glance is a very attractive woman slim figure blond hair dark brown eyes, her lips thin and cruel looking, she rarely shows emotion except anger but it is when you look into those dark brown eyes they reflect hard as granite and with more of a touch of insanity, cruel as to eat a mans soul.

The front door bursts open and her husband Ben comes rushing in cursing with a telegram in hand entering the parlor he pours a big shot of whiskey and drops into a big over stuffed chair he then thrusts the telegram at her, she quickly grabs it from his hand her heart racing, as she feared it is from her cousin Drew, "JOE DEAD, MOUNTIE HAS PACKAGE HEADING TO CALGARY ADVISE CONTACT YUMA ADAMS- DREW"

"Ben go find Yuma tell him this job pays top dollar and I would like to see him pronto, if that damn Mountie gets to Calgary we are done for we have to get Joe's gold then it will be my great pleasure in killing the little bitch, thinks herself so special. I will watch the life drain from those beautiful blue eyes, now damnit get a move on, damn you men cannot get anything right."

Duff is nearly finished packing supplies for the trail when the telegraph comes clicking to life with Inspector Steele's reply, "SGT FLEMING A PROMISE MADE MUST BE KEPT, CONTINUE WITH HASTE TO CALGARY-ON ARRIVAL CONTACT JUDGE HARMEN HATHAWAY, GOOD LUCK." The Inspector is known far and wide to be a hard man but an hombre who understands and enforces the code, Duff has heard of Judge Hathaway a good man but real fire eater and a man consumed by not so much the law but justice a damn fine man but a bad enemy no fear or backup in the man. The Sgt leaves his Scarlet tunic and service revolver on his bunk this now is a personal matter and he will treat it as such he is now dressed in a light blue shirt and buckskin jacket a black bandana around his neck and to top it off he wears his well worn beat up grey Stetson hat. From a peg above his cot he removes his gun belt and straps it around his waste, in the leather holster against his thigh is a .45 calibre Smith and Wesson Schofield a heavy hard hitting smoke wagon, the leather sheath on the back of the gun belt holds a prized Spanish Muela knife 8 inches of razor sharp Spanish steel with a bone handle, Duff paid dearly for it but the blade kept him alive through 2 wars, even in the day of gun law it still often comes down to men with nerve and cold steel.

The last thing the Sgt does before leaving the shack is to write a note for his 2 Constables advising them of his absence and to carry on with their assigned duties, gear in hand he steps out into the bright sun and with no surprise sees Mato sitting on his big buckskin horse waiting patiently, walking he walks over and shakes his friends hand. "Glad you could make it so fast Brother, but I must warn you that we will be out numbered and out gunned, there seems to be a need to stop me from reaching Calgary. Now this is not a Mountie matter and I ask you as a friend but if you are smart you will turn around and ride out good chance both of us might be seeing the Great Spirit soon, but if your coming I need you to find us a route which gives us our best chance on busting through." The Sioux warrior gives off a grunt sort of chuckle amused by his friend, "It is good we ride and fight Brother, the wolf has been asleep to long and is ready for battle, may our medicine be strong and take many scalps, we ride when you are ready, you better have lots of coffee and sugar or I might change my mind, I will guide you now Red Coat we go." Smiling Duff climbs into the hurricane deck and shoves the Winchester into the boot then like a couple of youngsters let out some whoops and hollers as they thunder away from the post dust hanging in the air behind them. Both men are fully aware of the danger that waits for them Duff understands the job is to get Joe's gold to his young Granddaughter but if it comes to a scrap they will show the enemy how men of war fight and die theirs will not be the only blood soaking into the dry prairie grass.

Yuma Adams smiles to himself as he sips the excellent scotch whiskey from Ben's private stock while listening to Abby the hard hearted bitch tell him what she wanted from him and his men. He waits patently for her to finish then takes a good pull on the scotch giving him time to think over the proposal, finishing the drink he puts the glass on the desk then lights up a cigar before speaking. "So cousin Drew and his Black riders came up short no big surprise I doubt if those boys could catch a cold, they are to Eastern you should have called me in first, now my cut will be 20 percent killing a Mountie is bad medicine and this Mountie Fleming is a ring tailed terror in a fight and he will probably have that damn Sioux Mato with him who has killed more white men than the plague." I got me 8 tough hardcases and get cousin Drew and his men to meet us at Three Hills makes it an even dozen but this is going to get bloody both those assholes are iron on iron hard and will make a fight of it. Well Abby do we have a deal if so me and the boys will be on the trail within 2 hours." Abby is furious 20 percent there is no way this hired gunman is getting any of her money promises can be broken and accidents happen, "Yuma you have us over a barrel, we both know 20 percent is what to high but I am not greedy 80 percent is a hell of a lot better than nothing, once the Brat Miss Tracey has her tragic accident Ben and I are off to New York then Europe. I am leaving this god forsaken wilderness and never coming back do whatever you have to and kill anyone who tries to stop you, now get the hell out of my house."

The next morning one of the local boys delivers a telegram to Judge Harmen Hathaway he knew at once it must be important because Inspector Steele did not waste much money on telegraph messages, his smile grows as he reads the short message its intent clear keep Miss Tracey Dobson alive and safe from harm until Sgt Fleming makes contact. Judge Hathaway knows of the underhanded and evil deeds of Ben and Abby and dearly wants them in the hoosegow but never can get a live witness or enough evidence he is going to really enjoy this. Judge Hathaway is an old time, common sense judge who was at one time town Marshal, Deputy Sheriff, Railroad Detective and lawyer before taking up the gavel, in the early rough years his big English bulldog revolver was always close at hand, the judge ran a tight courtroom. Telegram in hand he puts on his coat and big western hat he then goes back to his desk and slips a short barrelled .38 revolver in his coat pocket, always be prepared snakes come in all shapes and sizes, whistling to himself he leaves his office to pay a call on Ben and Abby Weatherby.

Tracey Dobson sits on the bed in her room on the second story of her Aunt Abby's house, a beautiful young woman of 18, long yellow hair and blue smiling eyes nice trim figure but today her eyes do not smile she is frightened she has not heard from her grandfather he should be back by now or at least sent word. She fears for him he is the only person in the world who she loves and is loved back, Aunt and Uncle Weatherby frighten her they never make any direct threats but there is menace a bullying in what was not said, vile, her movements very restricted like the bird in a gilded cage. She fears deeply if she does not escape soon they mean to do her harm, well one thing sure she is Joe's Granddaughter and a fighter, Joe is a skilled fighter with about any weapon including his hands and feet and iron on iron hard, they come for her she will fight and fight hard.

Minutes later she hears her Aunt speaking with someone at the front door after a few minutes of conversation her Aunt in her sickly fake sweet voice asks her to come down and join them in the sitting room they have a quest. After quickly fixing her hair and smoothing out her skirt with her hands she hurries down the stairs, entering she sees an elderly tough looking gentlemen in a store bought suit sitting in one of the overstuffed chairs she knew to be Judge Hathaway. Her Aunt and Uncle are both standing and are looking uncomfortable and a bit confused by the Judges unannounced visit. The Judge invites Tracey to sit in the chair beside him he has some news for her and she must be strong, "Miss Tracey I hate to be the one bringing you the news but your Grandfather Joe is dead he was killed by a gang of outlaws out to steal his gold, but old Joe was to tough and western for them although shot twice he evaded his killers until a North West Mounted Police Sgt found him as he was breathing his last. The Sgt. has taken possession of Joes gold and has promised the old man that he will get your inheritance to you or die trying. "I know Sgt Fleming he is a man of his word and experienced warrior fighting overseas and hard as they come and he will have to be because some unknown people have sent hired killers out to stop the Sgt he will have a hard dangerous journey but I have every confidence good shall prevail." Now while we wait for the Mountie I am concerned with your safety with so much money involved so as of this minute I rule that you are now under my protection which means your are under the Alberta Governments protection, and that means if anyone and I mean anyone that does you harm will be in my court and I will hang them without hesitation or remorse." The Judge chose his words carefully so Abby and Ben got the full impact of his message and he is not kidding justice will be served, "Miss Tracey myself or the Marshal shall call on you every morning to make sure you have no concerns and if there is anything you need just ask your Aunt she will be happy to oblige her niece, and I am at your command day or night. Sorry about old Joe him and I go way back to our riding days at 40 dollars a month and found, honey your Grampa was one of the good ones and will be remembered fondly. "Well I must be running you folks have a big sky day now, see you tomorrow Miss Tracey." Leaving the Weatherby house the Judge is feeling a sense of satisfaction he has not felt in a long time, and he knows that Abby's greed will lead her and her coyote of a husband to prison or the noose and he surely hopes it is his gavel that hammers home their fate.

Abby's rage burns like hellfire that damn meddling Judge he could be trouble everything depends on Yuma and Drew to get the gold and kill that damn Mountie she knows it is an all in game now but she is confident when the gun smoke clears she will have Joe's gold and fully intends leaving her useless husband holding an empty sack. He can take the 13 steps to the long drop into hell, very soon now she will be free from her wilderness prison, dinner at Delmonico's in New York city fills her crazed mind with fantasy.

CHAPTER 4

AMBUSH

Duff and Mato set an easy pace it is a good 4 day ride to Calgary with some rough country and badlands to get through and just for fun somewhere up ahead there are an unknown number of hardened killers heading to intercept them. Duff knows he and Mato will need every bit of skill and luck to get through the killing blockade but one thing sure those Lads want to battle they will be facing maybe the most dangerous Sioux warrior of the plains. Myself a member of the famous Scottish Fleming fighting clan, fighting skills inherited through generations of Fleming warrior men who are known to fight hard and die harder.

Mato decides even though a big longer and a rougher trail to stay to move northwest staying in the foothills close to the mountains then turn south taking them into Cow town, Duff figured out quickly his friends plan and agrees. This will be their best chance, but on the other hand there are places they will be riding through where you can hide a small army, ambush is a strong possibility, well he thinks to himself smiling, might be a damn fine scrap. The decision made Mato leads off north Duff behind with the packhorse although there is little chance of danger yet both men have their long guns out and are ready for bear, fate will now decide how the journey ends.

Yuma Adams after departing the Weatherby house walks directly over to the Single Spur saloon entering he spots his second in command Silver Spikes and tells him to round up the men and meet him at the livery stables bring their gear they have a job and they would be riding within the hour. Without waiting for a response he leaves and once on the street walks over to the general store for supplies and extra ammunition, you never want to get caught short on ammo Canadian wilderness. The game is afoot Yuma has no plans on ever giving the gold to Abby that crazy bitch he knows Drew and his Black Riders aim to kill him and anyone who try for the prize. Once the Mountie is dead and the gold is his hands Drew and his Black Riders are no longer of use and their carcasses will be left for the carrion and their bones will bleach in the hot summer sun. His men will see to that, but he knows not to underrate cousin Drew he has the instincts of a coyote and will kill without remorse. While waiting for the boys to arrive Yuma rolls himself a quirley and fires it up taking the harsh smoke deep into his lungs, the smoking helps him think, one thing sure he does not like the idea of going after a Mountie and especially this Mountie, Duff is a known man and proved himself smart capable and wang leather strong, does not know how to step back, and that damn Mato may be even more deadly but with. Yuma is uneasy though he has a dozen hard killers against the 2 of them there can only be one outcome, but the hired killer feels uneasy as if deaths icy fingers are reaching for him, he then sees the boys coming and shakes the dark thoughts away, time for war talk and travel.

All of Yuma's gunmen are ex soldiers mostly cavalry except for the mixed breed Black Feather born of French father Cree mother not accepted by either of his people he has become bitter and burns with hatred for just about everything except killing his only perverted pleasure. Only by being one of the best scouts in the west gets him riding with Yuma and his night riders and he just happens to be real handy with a rifle. Yuma snubs out his quirley with the toe of his boot and begins to tell his men about the job and about Drew and the Black Riders, he gives his best man Silver Spikes the job of keeping an eye on cousin Drew but they all will be watching for trouble. After the meeting breaks up the men separate to prepare all being old hands at their trade were ready in no time and 40 minutes later 9 deadly killers ride north out of Calgary towards the rendezvous at Three Hills then the hunt for their prey begins with the prize a golden treasure.

Drew curses wondering how his ear can hurt even though it is no longer there, damn it hurts he is going to skin the Mountie before he kills him, Yuma and his men should be arriving soon he knows after getting the gold Yuma must die quick it will be kill or be killed the curse of the shiny soft metal. It brings out the worst in people corrupting minds feeding greed like a starving animal, the Natives are much wiser when it comes to gold if you cannot eat it or it has no useful purpose for helping a person survive then it is of little use and for the most part have very little interest in it. Damn Abby it will be no easy thing keeping the gold from Yuma or for that matter just staying alive after this is finished he is getting as far away from his insane cousin as he can and with luck never cross paths with her again, the sound of horses brings him back to reality looks like the time for thinking is over Yuma and his men are riding into camp.

Silvers Spikes with is warped sense of humor asks Drew, "I swear boys didn't old Drew here have 2 ears last time we met you recon one is enough do you haha, so do you care to share the tale of your missing ear looks damn sore." Drew red faced and shamed reluctantly told the boys a close version of what happened seems he got tougher and meaner in his storytelling but he told them how Sgt Fleming snuck up on them and killed Rowdy Pepper and shot his ear off. Now he is looking forward to the next meeting and hopes he gets him alive have Black Feather work on him keeping him alive begging for death. Yuma gets serious now and tells the pack, "now you men listen close I am only going to say this once I am running the show and you will follow my orders I will kill any man that disobeys, now they are only 2 men but they may be the most skilled and deadly fighters anywhere to be found, you all know Mato so I need not tell you how dangerous that damn Sioux is but it is old Duff that worries me he fought in many wars on the other side of the ocean. He has commanded armies, has many medals for his bravery, he is a master at both gun and knife but not afraid to go skull and knuckle, Duff Fleming is wang leather tough and even dead he will find some way to take you down with him, boys I recon it is going to get hotter than a whorehouse on nickel night before its done. "Ok men mount up we can get a couple hours ride before we camp, Black Feather scout ahead and look for a good campsite, now you lazy bastards mount up and let's ride."

Duff is pleased they are making good time and the horses are holding up well, an incident happened that morning that still has the Mountie smiling, it was just after sunrise and they had only been on the trail a short while when suddenly 6 young Sioux warriors appear over a rise and with screams and war cries charge at the 2 riders, Mato smiles and tells the Mountie to stay where he is and then rides out about 20 yards and stops rifle in hand barrel pointing at the sky. A Sioux warrior is a pleasure to watch, true horse people and riders to match any in the world the Sg watches fascinated knowing he is extremely lucky to see some true wild Indians, the war cries louder now and then the warriors recognize the man waiting as Mato then it was pure chaos and comic. It was like them boys ran into a wall, dust flying nervous yelling then 6 young warriors ride 6 different directions horses full out as if the spirit Unk Cekula was chasing them. Like the scout and killer Jerry Potts, Mato is known by everyone Indian and White as a man not to be trifled with and have their graveyards to prove it, the 2 men exchange a good laugh and are back on the trail. Both men once again serious they know the closer they get to Calgary the more likely an attack or ambush, Duff looks to his friend thinking he could think of no better man he would rather have fighting at his side.

While saddling up in the pre dawn light the Mountie calculates the distance to Calgary and figures 20 to 25 miles he is grim and dark like the morning he is sure that the fight will be today and neither he or Mato are under any illusions that the their hunters would be many and all killers desperate gold feverish men. A smile once again crosses his lips he has faced great odds before and survived the warrior blood of his ancestors now pumps hot through his body, now it is time to get er done. Both men ride without talking Mato studying the ground for sign and Duff watching the landscape from a distance black Feather watches the riders with an evil sneer he praises himself on how well he has set up the ambush. Knowing his prey would suspect them to ambush them in the hills and Mato was sure to spot the trap, instead he had men dig shallow trenches about a foot deep behind rocks, sagebrush and any other cover both men would be dead before they can hear the gunshots. Yuma likes his scouts plan and is settled in nicely hidden behind a large stone his and Drew's men were all in place and well hidden it will not be long now and with the Mountie and Drew dead he will be rich, now the waiting and Yuma hates waiting.

Mato suddenly pulls up and dismounts then pretending he is checking a front hoof of his horse he tells the Mountie is fairly sure he saw movement and the reflection off a rifle barrel just ahead and off to the left behind a large clump of sagebrush, Duff the dismounts and begins to check his horses hooves knowing better just takes a quick glance across the whole area, both men know this is it for both would have set their ambush here as well, always do the unexpected. Duff is back in the hurricane deck pulls out his sack of tobacco and papers and while rolling a couple of quirley's looks around desperately for an escape route. Their enemies have set the trap well anyway the Sgt looked at it they would have to run the gauntlet of hot lead and gun smoke but they were going to charge on their own terms. Just before they get in good rifle range they are going to split right and left and charge the pack of killers with a little luck they may get behind them before the polecats are ready. Mato and he talk it over briefly and agree on the plan of attack wishing each other luck they ride slowly forward then at around 200 yards both men dig the spurs in and split up going full gallop, rifle shots can now be heard Duff hears a bullet zip by his ear sounding much like a bee, the reins around his saddle horn and riding with his knees the

Mountie begins returning fast and accurate fire. He can hear Mato's Henry rifles bark, he is closing on the ambushers when a man rises suddenly from the ground beside him to pull him from his horse but a slash across the face with the hot gun barrel ended that.

The fighting now is close and desperate Duff feels hot lead rip through his thigh the bullet goes straight through and into his horse which goes down in a heap holding tightly on his rifle the Mountie rolls away from the dying horse dust clouds his vision then the Mountie is hit by a second big slug this time deep into the left lower side of his stomach, Duff is hit hard and knows it. He keeps fighting worry about his wounds later, damn getting hot with lead flying everywhere. Moving the rifle to his left hand he draws the Schofield and cuts loose taking out 2 of the enemy with the heavy revolver he no longer hears Mato's rifle firing no time to think of that now for he is looking directly into the eyes of cousin Drew, "I got you now you son of a bitch I am going to blow your guts…, "Drew's speech is interrupted by the hot lead fired from the hip by the Mounties rifle tears the killers throat open almost decapitating him, Duff knew he was near his limit he must get away fighting a rear action he fights his way into the hill using every bit of cover. Safe for the moment he looks back at the field of battle and with great sadness sees his friend is down and not moving 5 dead men surround him, the survivors continue to hammer bullets into him, Black Feather now wants his prize the Great Mato's scalp will make a fine trophy, he rushes to the fallen man scalping knife ready. Black Feather looks down at Mato not so tough now he thinks to himself, Mato was all talk leaning over the Sioux he reaches over the man to grab his hair in shock he sees Mato's eyes then feels the searing pain of the Sioux's knife being driven upwards into his throat through his mouth and deep into his brain stopping at the top of his skull, death was quick, Mato smiles and breaths his last.

Knowing he can do nothing for his friend the Mountie moves deeper into the hills hoping to find shelter and water to tend his wounds it was still 20 hard miles to Calgary wounded or not he must not quit to quit is to die and his promise must be kept no matter the price even if it means his life.

CHAPTER 5

DIGGING DEEP

Yuma's eyes open staring into the endless blue of the big western sky he is having trouble seeing out of his right eye it feels sticky awake his head throbs the killer gently touches the side of his scalp he almost screams with pain his fingers coming away covered in blood then the memories of the fight begin to come back to him. Slowly he sits up and looks around his eyes seeing his mind disbelieving, the first thing to catch his attention is the death embrace of Mato and Black Feather he shudders at the sight of the big knife stuck into his dead scouts throat. Mato was the wolf today and died fighting many of his men are dead Silver died hard trying to hold his guts in a sharp stab of pain smashes through his skull he remembers now the Mountie savagely smashing him in the head with the hold barrel of his long gun, damn that man now where the hell is he?

The wounded Mountie is in a bad way desperately in need of water and to tend to his wounds and plan his next move he does know one thing for a certain fact if he does not get himself a horse he will not make Calgary and will die alone in the western wilderness. Fighters like Sgt Fleming accept early on one day this fate waited for most men who live by the sword, but now water, then he heard it a bee, bees never go far from water but he did not see what direction it flew he sits and waits. Not more than 30 seconds pass another bee fly by this time he sees it flying towards some tall green grass unable to stand Duff crawls on his hands and knees his breath coming hard in gasps near the end of his rope the Sgt gives off a smile as his hand settles in cool wet mud. Slowly he moves forward through the tall grass and finds a small pool of fresh water fed from an underground spring, he knows he is taking a risk drinking with a belly wound but he is dehydrated and must have water he sticks his face deep into the cool pond and drinks deeply. Almost immediately he can feel life and energy returning to his battered and bruised body his body craves more water he knows he cannot drink to much it will make him sick, with effort Duff sits up not liking the idea he must see how bad he is hit gritting his teeth knowing the pain to come he lifts his blood soaked shirt he almost faints. The fabric separates from his skin, Duff has seen all sorts of wounds over the years and knew there impact it only took him a glance to know he is hurt bad.

Yuma still in a bit of shock counts how many of his men survived only himself and 4 men remain alive but one has a nasty shoulder wound, the only good thing about this whole affair is that the Mountie did him a favour by filling cousin Drew full of lead saving him the trouble. He now thinks to himself this might just work out in I get the Mountie and kill his remaining men a man good live real good for a long time with that much gold. One of the men hands him a canteen after taking a long drink he washes his face with his hands getting the sticky and crusted blood off his eye, damn his head hurts that damn Mountie is going to pay a hard price for disfiguring him. Taking a cigar from his vest pocket he fires it up and after taking a couple deep drags to calm himself he orders 2 of his men to go get the horses and the other men to check the dead men for any valuables and ammunition, head throbbing the outlaw leader sits smoking waiting for the men to get back, one of his men tells him old Duff took some lead soon the hunt will start again.

Duff checks out the wound in his thigh but lucky it went clean through and did not hit bone or artery it is not even bleeding much so he ignores it concentrating on the stomach wound, frustrated he gives off a low sounding curse of helplessness. The bullet has gone in to deep to try and get it out the only thing he can do is cut strips off his buckskin jacket and tie them tightly around his stomach covering the ugly looking wound. Now laying on his back hat over his eyes to shield the bright sun the Sgt starts pondering on the best way to get himself a horse, his war blood has now cooled is replaced by sadness at the thought of his good friend and warrior Brother laying dead on the dry earth his blood taken greedily but the thirsty soil. Along with the sadness is great pride on how bravely Mato fought this is how it should be with warriors die fighting the good fight as his friend said often "It is a good day to die."

Sgt Fleming jumps instinctively as hot breath on his face his eyes open and looks directly into the big nostrils of a horse slowly he moves hand to grab the reins his voice low and calm not to spook the animal with great relief his hand holds the leather straps, the animal puts up no resistance actually seems to be happy to have some company, horses by nature are not solitary creatures by habit and need companionship even if it is human. Duffs weary brain begins to function after splashing some water on his face, he realizes he had passed out for a fair spell because it was full dark with the moon high in the sky now, the Mountie struggling uses the stirrup to pull himself up then moves in front of his new companion and places his forehead on the horses head stroking its neck he begins to talk to him. "Laddie you are the most beautiful horse in all of the world and I thank all the Saints for your timely deliverance, now my brother I must apologize for what I must do to you this ride could mean both our deaths but all must be given I will ride you hard and you my beautiful brother will be your very best today. We must be strong hard today, rest now my beauty we leave soon please forgive me." The wounded Mountie stays standing leaning against the horse which in reality was far from beautiful, some sort of wild mustang cross thin stringy main and a thin rat tail, but he also had a thick toughness about him Duff figures him like himself a bruiser, today he is sure they are going to have to prove it.

Yuma curses and talking to no one in particular says, "now were the hell could that damn Mountie get to how far could he get with no horse I recon there is a good chance he cashed in his chips now spread out we are not leaving without the gold". The man with the shoulder wound is in a bad way and will not live to see Calgary good he thinks one less to kill but now they are down to 4 fighting men and not his best by far, Damn that mountie. Minutes later the morning silence is broken by one of his men yelling and pointing ahead where a horse and rider can be seen just going over a small ridge, smiling now he lets out a whoop and digs in his spurs, Yuma yells to the men," Ok boys first man who bring the Mountie down gets a 500 dollar bonus no lets go kill this son of a bitch."

Sgt Fleming curses his luck a mere 10 seconds more and he would have got away unseen now the deadly chase is on seems death does ride a horse, ahead about a mile is a nice high piece of ground a good place to take out one or 2 with his rifle he knows he has to bring the odds down. His aim better be true he has only 3 cartridges left for his Winchester after that he is down to his Schofield and knife, slapping his horse on the ass with his hat and digging in spurs he lets the horse cut loose. Never judge a book by its cover this big jughead horse was all horse much faster than expected and had plenty of bottom they fly across the flat prairie getting to his ambush spot well ahead of his pursuers the Mountie more falls than climbs out of the saddle his insides burning like hellfire. He knows from experience he is loosing to much blood and making him weak, slowly leaning on the animal he leads it to a spot out of the line of fire and ties off the reins. Duff can now see the riders in the distance he has to find a good spot soon they would be in rifle range soon sweat stings his eyes making them water, he makes his call and holding tight his stomach and growling in pain he moves to where he would shoot from slowly and with agony lowers himself to prone position he then levers a big shell into the chamber snugs the butt to his shoulder and waits.

Yuma sees one of his men knocked from the saddle before he hears the sound of the shot, the next bullet came so close to him the friction of it burns his cheek with disbelief he sees another of his men sway them fall from the saddle, not wasting any time he and his last man ride hell for leather out of rifle range not knowing the Mountie is now out of shells. With the rifle now empty Duff begins the long painful crawl back to his horse, he suddenly comes awake with a start he had passed out again but only for a few seconds cursing himself for his weakness he finishes his brutal short crawl after a couple deep breaths and using the empty rifle he gets to his feet. With one all or nothing move Duff gets his leg over the saddle and is now sits weaving in the hurricane deck, red/black pain explodes into his very soul so intense he nearly weeps. Satisfied he will not fall out of the saddle he points his horse in the general direction of Calgary and puts the horse into a ground eating trot, to take his mind off the pain the Mountie concentrates on his next course of action only 2 man hunters left but he knew he knew the reality that he will have to kill these men if he has any chance of making Cow town and keeping his promise to Joe. The horse is tiring and stumbles the Mountie screams in pain but somehow manages to stay in the saddle the time has come he would make his stand on the next rise on the trail that way the riders are below him, he pulls out his big revolver and makes sure it is fully loaded and returns it to its holster, holding tight to the saddle horn he rides grimly towards his chosen destination.

Yuma is confused by what he sees, the Mountie standing dead centre in the middle of the trail with only his six gun in hand, he and his last man talk it over and decide the Mountie is done in and making his last stand. Yuma tells his last man it is time to end it they will use their rifles and ride him down pound his carcass into the ground both men fully load their rifles and together charge at the gallop towards the man standing on the hill. Sgt Fleming is now only standing because of his damn Scottish stubborn heritage and wonders to himself how many of his ancestors went out this way smiling he thinks not a bad way better go out fighting like the wolf than slaughtered like a sheep, he sees the men riding towards him rifles blasting hot lead and death. Bullets kick up dirt all around him, calmly Sgt Fleming stands sideways takes a dueling stance, the Schofield .45 is a hard hitting gun, hits with a punch like a red hot sledgehammer, the big gun barks and bucks in his hand 4 times, seconds later 2 riderless horses fly by him, Yuma made his play and lost.

Judge Hathaway is sitting in front of his office on main street Calgary when he sees a lone rider coming down the street towards him on a very tired horse covered in lather the rider head down sways back and forth in the saddle suddenly it occurs to him this must be Sgt Fleming. Leaving his chair he rushing into the street to intercept the rider the town doctor and Marshal join him in the street, the Judge grabs the reins the horse, "Sgt Fleming well done man we were worried about you when you were overdo come man lets get you some food and coffee. "The Doc looks to the judge and in a soft voice says to him, "Sorry Judge the man cannot hear you he is dead."

A PROMISE IS A DEBT UNPAID- ROBERT W SERVICE

STORY 7

REMEMBER SOME THING ARE NOT FOR SALE

CHAPTER 1

THE THREAT

Sean Murphy is an Irish horse trader and is known throughout the land to have only the very best horses for sale his family from the Kilkenny County in the Emerald Isle has been breeding champion horses for over 200 years. Sean being a man of courage and vision brought a stallion and 4 mares across the seas 16 years ago to make his fortune in the new lands and truth be known he pretty much has with secret bank accounts in New York and Chicago life is good for Sean but we all know the only constant in life is change and Squire Murphy's world is about to get ugly, bloody and dangerous.

Sean is a travelling trader moving from city to city his travels have lead him today by a small river on the outskirts of Baton Rouge Louisiana, in all of the vast country there is no city like Baton Rouge, a mixture of English, French and Spanish, every sort of commerce a money town and money like a magnet it draws all forms of evil men, thieves, bunko artists, pick pockets, killers, thugs and card sharps and gangs. The most professional and dangerous group of river rats is lead by one man with absolute power and control named Ox Boucher a huge man standing 6 ft 4 in his socks and at least 240 pounds of muscle and sinew, he had no real neck with hugs shoulders and ham sized fists, loved knuckle and skull scraping it excited him to feel a mans bones snap with his immense strength, mean clean through. Ox and his thugs had a percentage of every piece of action in town and all store owners were paying him protection money which meant they paid Ox not to burn down the store or they take beating, the big man and his leg breakers were doing very well always lots of money for some bonded rum and whores, Ox was content then he saw the horse.

The horse that caught the gangsters eye is Divano named after an Irish war god, Divano is and Irish draught horse mixed with a champion warmblood making him a versatile, intelligent and horse for good temperament if left be, the stallion stands 6'2 at the shoulder and his coat is blacker then coal in a mineshaft the only color a splash of white in the rough form of a star on his forehead. The beautiful horses breeding goes back generations and the old country there is no finer animal around and the showoff Divano knows it. To the pleasure of his friend and human brother Sean Murphy, Sean was there when the foal was born, and they have been together ever since developing a close bond. Sean has had many offers to buy Divano but he feels it would be like selling his brother or one of his family this horse will never be for sale at any price, but Sean makes good money from stud fees and his prices high you want the best you have pay for it. The horse trader never travels with more than 10 horses more would be to hard to manage even with his vaquero wrangler Adolfo but people who knew horseflesh will pay dearly for a Murphy horse. Adolfo was no longer young sneaking up on 60 a thin man all muscle and sinew, tough as wang leather, he and Sean have been together for just over 10 years and make a good team, Adolfo had a gift when coming to horses best trainer Sean has ever come across, not so many years back Adolfo was know as the Ghost because he was the best horse thief in Mexico been known to have stolen horses from Apaches and brother that is not easy to do and damn dangerous.

Early the next afternoon Sean was enjoying a beautiful day sitting in the cool shade when he sees to big hard looking men approaching his caravan he smiles to himself he knows paid muscle when he sees it this should be interesting he rise from his chair to greet his visitors, "Good afternoon gentlemen I am Sean Murphy and if you are here to purchase a fine animal you are in the right place now laddies how can I help you?" "The bigger of the thugs has on a brown beat up derby hat he speaks for them, "Mister our boss Ox Boucher sent us over to buy and bring that big black stud horse you got in the back the boss says he will give you 500 dollars for him, it is much more that the plug is worth, now get him ready we will take him with us." Sean his Irish temper up, plug indeed looking back at the men his look is now hard and his voice low and menacing, "You punks go back and tell your boss Divano is not for sale at any price would be like selling a member of my family, boyos I will not discuss the matter further I have 10 fine horses here that are for sale and he would be wise to chose any of them, now you lads run back to your boss." The man in the bowler hat could not believe his ears is this man insane Ox will have him skinned and nailed to the barn door, "Horse trader we are leaving with that horse even if it means stepping over your dead body, now get the hell out of way or pay the piper." Just then the unmistakeable sound of a shotgun hammer being pulled back is heard the 2 bruisers look over at Adolfo his black eyes shining his smile wide and firmly in his grip is a double barrel 10 gauge shotgun basically a small cannon, men may take a chance with a rifle or barking irons but never a shotgun especially a 10 gauge. The 2 thugs are at least smart enough to know when to pull in their horns one look into the old Mexicans eyes told them one wrong move and he would cut them in half before leaving bowler hat has a few final words. "Murphy you are making a big mistake Ox owns this town and he always gets what he wants, he will come for you and he will kill you and knowing him might just shoot the horse out of spite, you and the Mexican are dead men." Sean had enough in a rough voice tells the men to get and if big scary Ox wants him he will be easy to find, the men turn and leave talking and shaking their heads no one likes giving bad news to the Ox, can be bad for your health.

CHAPTER 2

THE BAIT AND SWITCH

Sean with a grim look watches the thugs walk away he knows this is just the beginning Ox has to get Divano now or it will show him to be weak and threaten his hold over his victims, Sean goes to his caravan and reaches under his bed with a sigh he pulls out a bottle of fine Irish whiskey time to go visit his old friend Alverez Jones. Alverez has a livery stable on the near edge of the city, as with most men in Baton Rouge Alverez has a past of blood and killing but old Alverez always did his killing from the front. Now he just keeps to himself running the livery and playing poker at night, Sean needs a favor from his old friend and Alverez does love for good whiskey. The 2 men go back a ways first meeting as NCO.s in General Bufford's Cavalry fighting shoulder to shoulder, when the slaughter finally ended the men separated Sean went back to Ireland and brought back Billy Jack a fine Irish draft horse and 4 beautiful warmblood mares to start the horse trading, Divano has the hot blood of Billy Boy running through his veins. Alverez having great skill with guns began selling his fighting skills in a couple cattle wars, town enforcer, and at times a bandit in those days he was known throughout the west as the Hammer.

The 2 men meet with western good humour and only insults old soldiers would share, Alverez has Sean come back into the livery office before sitting he grabs 2 glasses and puts them on his old desk, he spotted the good hootch Sean brought right off, the men have a couple stiff shots and catch up like old friends do. After pouring the third Sean tells his meeting with the Ox's 2 henchmen and that he suspected an attempt will be made to steal Divano and he needs a favor, he lays out his plan to the livery man who upon hearing it gives off a big laugh and readily agrees to help telling Sean he hates Ox and has to use a lot of restraint bot to belly shoot the big son of a bitch, "Sean my old friend I have just what you need and will be there just after dark now I will be coming in from the trees just east of your campsite, damn boy about time there was some action I am really going to enjoy this, now you cheap bastard pour me another drink damn fine whiskey I can almost smell the peat, damn its good to see you again Amigo." Finishing his drink Sean leaves the livery and reluctantly the bottle and goes back to the camp he and Adolfo have much to do and little time to do it, should be a damn interesting night.

Supper is finished it will be dark soon while some light remains Sean breaks down his Colt single action .45 calibre revolver with a 7 and a ½ inch barrel a deadly tool in the hands of a warrior such as the Irish horse trader. After cleaning and lightly oiling the smoke wagon he loads it with fresh shells then sticks in his belt for a quick belly draw, Adolfo just carries the 10 gauge damn thing is so big should have wheels, feeling all is ready he now sits and fires up a cigar and waits patiently for Alverez to put his plan into action. Out of the night comes the sound of an owl just at the spot Alverez said he was coming in they had been using the owl call as a signal every since they scouted for the great General, Sean in a low tone tells his friend all is quiet and to meet him where he has Divano secured and that Aldolfo has already left but would be back soon. Laughing softly they complete the preparations and with luck old Ox will have a fit and get mad, which is just what Sean wants men who live by the gun cannot afford to get mad leads to mistakes which puts your next stop on boot hill. A few minutes later the wrangler returns nods to the men the deed is done and takes up his position to wait now they all wait hidden and hope Ox takes the bait, Sean figured it would be awhile yet the thieves will probably wait until late hoping everyone is asleep, relieved about what Sean figures to be near 3 am the watchers hear sounds of tree branches rustling and feet approaching, these certainly ain't western men who learn stealth by fighting Indians like the Apache.

Sean and his 2 companions watch as 4 men thinking themselves sly sneak up slowly to where Divano is being held, the horse trader lets them come and waits until he is sure they got a firm grip on the horse then with a Rebel yell starts shooting holes in the night sky both Alverez and Aldolfo do the same once he sees the thieves leaving with the horse he flips open the cylinder of his barking iron and reloads best have a fully loaded weapon from here in. Ox is sitting on a stack of hay in his barn and getting angry, "where the hell are those dumb assholes and why was there so much shooting anything happens to my horse he will take someone's eyes", just then the barn door bursts open and his 4 men stumble terrified and panicked through leading a horse, relief settles in as they realized they made it with the horse and alive but the fear crashes back as they look at the horse they brought their deadly employer. For a moment Ox is too stunned to speak instead of the magnificent Divano the boys brought back a plug mare old plug mare named Molley, what they did not know is Divano is safe and sound in Alverez's stable. Realizing he had been had Ox in anger lashes out at the closed thief hitting him with a sledgehammer right hand smashing the mans skull blood flows from his ears, mouth and nose mercifully he dies quick, Ox does not blink an eye this will be an example for those who fail him, he tells the men to get rid of the body he was leaving and needs a drink.

A battle won does not mean the war is Sean knew Ox would come at him next force him into a fight hoping to kill him, then the horse would be his and he would show the people of Baton Rouge he was still the he wolf, never one to be on the defensive Sean decides he will seek out and challenge the king rat, time to end it once and for all.

CHAPTER 3

KNUCKLE AND SKULL

Looking out the saloon batwing doors Ox sees a crowd gathering by the notice board something has them all stirred up curious the Rat King sends one of his boys to go see what all the fuss is about, as soon as the townsfolk see the pug coming they break up and go their own way. Ox watches as his man snatches the paper from the wall and walks back to the saloon not looking happy, Ox sets himself at his favorite table and pours his first shot of red eye the messenger hands Ox the note which was addressed to him. He reads in stunned silence and disbelieve, how dare the Irish son of a bitch, he tells the men in the saloon to keep it down he is going read the note out it to them.

"Ox Boucher you are a coward sending thugs to do your dirty work, I told your men there are some things are not for sale now I must teach you a painful lesson. At 10 am this morning I will be waiting in front of Alverez's livery for you, it will be hand to hand unless you are afraid is so I will thrash you with any weapon, when you are beaten you and your den of thieves will leave town the people have had enough of you. Let's see if you are are all mouth and brag, I am going to pin your ears back you big asshole, signed Sean Murphy." Ox flies into a rage throwing chairs and tables wood breaks glass shatters, his anger so intense he is spitting drool and shouting curses and swears Sean Murphy is a dead man.

To those people that do not know the horse trader they think him crazy and it is plum suicide to fight the beast but there is much more to Mrs. Murphy's son than meets the eye. Although he does not look it Sean is just over 6 feet tall and weights around 190 pounds with big shoulders and stout strong legs not an ounce of fat on him, iron on iron hard with immense strength. Sean grew up fighting on the docks in Ireland learning every dirty trick in the book, his uncle schooled him in wrestling and boxing he was fortunate enough as a young man at sea have a Chinese man named Ling teach him Chinese fighting showed him how to use his opponents strength against him, where and how to hit or kick to inflict pain or damage being a quick study he learned his lessons well. With about an hour to wait Alverez arrives wearing his 2 gun rig, one tied to his thigh the other in a belly holster for a quick grab, he wore a clean shirt polished high topped riding boots, and a new blue bandana around his neck, today Baton rouge will meet the Hammer, with Adolfo shot gun in hand we slowly walk together down towards the stables.

When word got out of the upcoming fight saloon owners opened up for betting giving 10 to 1 odds on Ox, so far not a single person has put his money on the underdog horse trader, leaving Sean and his wrangler at the livery the Hammer makes his way directly to the Flying Pelican, Hammer slams down 5 gold eagles and says to the bookie, "I got a hundred dollars to put on Murphy 10 to 1 odds if you have the balls for it, you having any?" Confident the bookie takes the bet just as Alverez turns to leave he is stopped by an insult, "Well lookie here the livery man all dressed up and toting big guns, you some kind of bad man, shit shoveller maybe for fun I should just notch your ears." Hammer knows the voice a punk kid named Frisco figuring himself a gunfighter needs some kills to be known and the livery man is a good start, Hammer turns and faces the threat without speaking he just reaches down and takes the leather thong off the hammer of his peacemaker and waits for the kid to make his move. Frisco is scared this not how it is supposed to be why does he not talk or beg for his life, as with seeing Alverez for the first time he knows he is looking at death he knows he cannot back out and makes a grab for his smoke wagon his hand grabs the handle of the revolver and freezes now looking directly into the barrel of the Alverez's 6 gun hammer back death only a small squeeze away. It is almost time for the fight, the Hammer tells Frisco to remove his gun belt and hand it to the bartender and if they meet in the street the kid better cross over or he will shoot on sight, with that he leaves not looking back. As Frisco fumes and curses he hears a laugh from one of the back tables, a gambler with a reputation for an honest game and a quick draw laughs and tells Frisco, "Kid you have no idea how close you came to dying today, you may be the only person I know who crossed guns with the Hammer and live and boy I have seen his graveyards, "Frisco hearing the famous gunfighters name goes all pale and weak in the knees, to hell with this he is taking up a less deadly profession.

The whole town shuts down and heads for the livery to watch the brawl they know it will be historic a story to pass down through the generations, Sean is ready or hopes he is ready he knows any mistakes and Ox will either cripple or kill him. The horse trader knows he will be tested this day never had he fought a man this big or powerful, it will have to be skill that wins the day. Ox is ready to go and with blood in his eye calls across to Sean, "You made a big mistake horse trader I have never been beaten with my fists I am going to break you then shoot that damn horse once we come up to scratch no rules we fight until only 1 is left standing over the others dead body, you ready for some you dirty Irish paddy?" Sean says nothing he removes his shirt a few gasps can be heard when people see his heavily muscled arms and chest after putting on a pair of skin tight leather gloves to protect his gand and makes his way to the scratch mark.

Sean flexes his muscles and loosing up nears the scratch mark without warning Ox steps over the mark and sucker punches Sean with a very heavy left hook to the side of the head sending him heavily to the ground. Sean is out stunned for a couple seconds he does not move then with a groan and tremendous effort begins to push himself up, pure instinct drives him he is almost out Ox gives of a growl and closes in for the kill but instead of rolling away Sean rolls at Ox's legs knocking the big man to the ground, Sean rolls a couple more turns to get some distance from his opponent, still in a fog Sean more hears than sees the big mans rush to get his massive arms around Sean. Just as Ox is about to smash into him Sean throws the big man with a hip toss Ox hits the ground hard knocking the windout of him, Sean smiles he is back in the brawl. Ox is a brawler and uses intimidation and brute strength to win his fights he is about to find out how effective a skilled fighter is, both men close slowly again Ox lets go the big left hook but this time Sean goes under it and makes him pay with 2 heavy shots to the ribs, live bones crack. Ox moves away holding his side his confidence is being destroyed no man has ever hit him near as hard he will have to end it quickly, but the horse trader has other ideas he starts to attack, striking quick painful blows, Ox leaves himself wide open Sean throws a straight right hand from the shoulder which turns Ox's nose into a bloody pulpy mess making the big man step back. From that moment it is no longer a brawl it is a big man is being taken apart almost like surgery chopped down to size, Sean finishes him off with a left hand hard into Ox's solar plexus and a perfect right upper cut to the sweet spot on the big mans chin, Ox luckily did not feel the hard ground as his face slammed into it.

Cheers erupt as Sean stands a bit unsteady gasping for breath, his head throbs from the effects of the Ox,s heavy punch, Hammer with a dozen men behind him walk into the human circle and gives Ox,s men notice that they were to take their boss and then they are to be out of Baton Rouge by sunrise or they would be killed on sight, no quarter, then dismisses then with a wave like shooing a fly, Ox and his rat pack are finished and they know it. Sean stays in Baton Rouge another 4 days sells a couple fine mares and makes a handsome profit, he and his wrangler pack up and have the horses ready for travel Sean is riding Divano whistling an old Irish tune he turns his big horse north off to the next town and if lucky a new adventure.

IT IS NOT EVERYTHING IN LIFE THAT HAS ITS TICKET, SO MUCH. THERE ARE THINGS NOT FOR SALE- AGATHA CHRISTIE

STORY 8

KNOW WHERE TO DRAW THE LINE

CHAPTER 1

LAWLESS HONDO TEXAS

Hondo Texas is a very dangerous town in 1886, all law had been killed or run out, the criminal element controls the town mainly Bryce Grimm and his sidekicks Lefty Sanders and Pen Floyd, every man a vicious killer and first rate gun thrower. At present Grimm is satisfied with the free booze, food and women the Blue Ox saloon has to offer. I have seen this before power corrupts soon Grimm and his men will be taking what they want and after they take everything they will probably burn and haze the town then move on looking for their next prey, there is no pity or remorse in these hard men, steal the gold from their mothers teeth-assholes.

My name is Gabriel Deacon, most folks call me Gab but a few years back I was known as THE MAN FROM MUSTANG, my profession was hired gun and enforcer, mostly on the right side of the law, but I chose who I worked for and I never went against women or kids. My gun has taken the lives of 14 men and probably would have been many more but for the incident in Carson City, a very bad day. That fateful morning as I was walking across main street a couple cattle rustlers and thieves Jim and Dave Fowler open up on me lead snapping by my head, I cut loose with my .44 colt and kill both men I take a flesh wound in the calf of my leg, but bullets do not care what or who they hit laying in the street motionless is 5 year old Tommy Billings. Luck was with the boy although a pretty severe wound he would survive but 2 inches over and the boy would be dead, in that moment I swore never to use a 6 gun again, and then I met my love Deb and my life started feeling worth while Deb and I are very happily married and work as a junior partner in her fathers feed lot and store, I only bring my .45 colt peacemakers out to clean and oil them and to work the leather of the holster to keep the leather soft. Memories flood back when I touch the guns so powerful my hands shake and my stomach gets queasy, the thought of having to put them on again scares the hell out of me. I have come across this evil before and soon I will have to draw the line and strap on my smoke wagons to make sure if Bryce and bunch cut loose, I surely do wish there was someone else but the Rangers are a 2 days hard ride away. Most the townsmen are good brave men in their own right but few if any crossed six shooters or have the courage to stand up to it. For now I am going to watch and wait I have to think where it is I draw the line the idea of facing 3 ruthless killers alone scares me now because unlike my gunfighter days I now have something precious to loose my sweet and beautiful wife Deb.

When I arrive at the feed lot I find Tom Arnold my Father in Law sitting behind his beat up old desk coffee in hand and a worried look stamped on his unshaven face, I pour a mug of the hot black coffee. Tom likes his coffee strong horse shoe floating strong which suits me just fine, after sitting I pull one of my thin black Mexican cigars and strike a fire it up before speaking, "morning Boss you like breakfast vittles didn't settle proper, why the long face Tom?" Tom takes a moment to re light his blackened pipe, "Gabe it is the same thing everyone else in town is worried about Grimm and his crowd no one is same but it is Deb and the other gals I fear for those men across the street are scum and without conscious." Just then through the office window I see a couple of the town boys I know who I pay to help out if things get busy I quickly excuse myself and hurry outside to intercept the 2 lads, we both arrive at the same time and almost crash into each other, the boys are brothers Billy Sanders is 14 and his younger brother Trevor is 12, good boys with to much spirit for small town living. "Morning Buckaroos got some work for you if you are interested it pays 2 silver dollars for each of you but it is serious work and if you do not do exactly what I say I will tan your hides-no fooling, so you up for it." Billy the oldest talked for the boys I can see the excitement in his eyes they know this is something different and in a small town any diversion is good the boys readily agree and ask what they want have to do." Well said Pard, ok what I need you to do is watch the Blue Ox saloon and keep an sharp eye out for Bryce Grimm and his crowd if they leave the saloon and start trouble come get me pronto, also watch for any new faces coming into town, if word gets out this is an open town with no law killers and outlaws being hunted by the law will be thicker than ticks on a hound dog hiding out and laying low." "Now you boys listen real close now this is not a game and the treat is real, never doubt those men will kill you if you give them reason, so you will only watch and report, do not get to close to the saloon just make it look like you are just sitting around nothing to do, you are both smart and smart beats brawn every time, so boys do we have a deal if so you start work now." It is no surprise the brothers jump at the chance and were off in a flash, I go in to see Tom and tell him about hiring the brothers, nobody pays much attention to town kids making them perfect spies, Tom chuckles at the idea then goes to the wall and takes down his Winchester Yellow Boy .44 calibre rifle and gun cleaning kit and begins cleaning and oiling the weapon then loading it wit new shells he places it back on the wall, I begin to suspect this ain't Tom's first gun battle.

CHAPTER 2

ON THE PROD

The town is quiet this morning I recon Bryce and the boys had a bit too much bust skull whiskey and are nursing hangovers I hope they stay low and nurse them and it does not make them mean and looking for trouble never know with hard men. Deb tells me that she has some shopping to do and if I want to eat, I better take her this morning and she hates the idea of having to stay in the house or back yard, very independent woman my wife, part of her charm. With breakfast and coffee finished I tell my sweetheart that I am going to go and scout the town and check in with her Dad then I would be back to take her shopping once again gently but sternly reminding her not to leave the yard alone for any reason.

There are not many folks up and about yet as I round the corner stepping on to Main Street and find the brother spies waiting for me, I can see by their faces they have news and I don't figure it will be good news, Billy as usual speaks for the boys, "Morning Boss we have been watching close as you asked they are all still in the saloon but last evening old Jonny Bower left the saloon with a skin full and was in a talking mood, seems like a couple of the town rowdies and pure trash have signed up with Grimm and his bunch, you know them Gabe, Clem Allison and his cousin Mason Tate both mean clean through, other than that everything is quiet." I give the boys a smile, "Damn fine work men good to work with fellas I can count on, now today I want you to be extra careful if guns get pulled you get your asses off the street and I mean pronto, bullets don't care who or what they hit, ok Bill here is a silver dollar for each of you as half payment and you boys go see Frank the cook at the café and get breakfast tell cookie I will be in to pay him later, now git I got work to do." After leaving my spies I head directly to see Tom at the feedlot, I know he will have his paint peeling black brew hot and ready and damn I need a cup, 5 to 1 are not good odds not even if you are Hickok good.

Tom is behind his desk enjoying his morning pipe and Arbuckle's coffee poured I fire up a cigar and give him the low down then tell him I am off to get Deb to take her shopping and would be back in about before exiting the office I suggest to Tom to take the long gun off the wall rack and keep it close at hand I have the same feeling of danger as in hostile Indian country and things may happen quick, damn my luck. Deb is waiting by the front door wicker shopping basket over her arm, greeting her with some mock formality and a smile I offer her my arm now arm and arm we make our way the Miners grocery and hardware store Deb is in a happy mood just happy for the small distraction. Arriving at our destination I open the door for Deb just as she is about to enter she is roughly pushed aside by a surly Pen Floyd my hand flashes and grabs Pen by the shoulder I spin him and pull his hogleg from his holster and toss it down the street out of reach then I backhand the outlaw, "Floyd I have seen men hung for less for insulting a western woman, now you give my wife a sincere I am real sorry or I am going beat you within an inch of your life, so what will it be Pen I have little patience with assholes today." Pen smiles hugely not a nice smile more of I am going to enjoy kicking your teeth in smile, he considers himself a fighter and tough man, "Well I ain't saying sorry to that bitch wife of yours so lets get to it pumpkin roller time you were taken down a peg or two".

Keeping a close eye on Pen I move to the middle of the street the outlaw moves fast rushing in an throwing a wicked right hand roundhouse I go under it and make him pay with a heavy kidney shot Pen lets out a grunt of pain, more careful now he circles and closes looking for an opening stepping back my foot slips on a loose rock of balance Pen pounces and gets in a couple hard shots to my head. My ears are ringing but I regain my balance and step forward throwing a straight right jab that breaks and bloodies Pen's nose. Screaming in pain and fury Pen rushes in swinging, enough is enough time to see who is the better man I take my stance and we go toe to toe, no defence we hit and slug until one of us drops, I can feel Pen's punches loosing their power he takes his first step back. I do not let up I hit him with everything but he outhouse and like a tree I chop him down until he lays motionless and bleeding in the dusty street. My breath comes in gasps my tired muscles weak and shaking, I look up at Deb her face white with shock at the unleashed violence but as a fine western woman gathers herself and enters the store to complete her errands, I see Billy and Trevor and wave them over to me, "Got another job for you and it needs to be done quiet and quick, first go find the Mayor and Tom at the feed store and have them meet me at the town Marshal's office and they need to enter by the rear door I will meet them there as soon as I get the wife home, then it is back to sentry duties, any questions you young hellions?"

The young brothers are loving the intrigue and being a part of it now moving into the back alley they go about their task unseen, as I wait for the wife to finish her errands I make my decision this is where I must draw the line with my thrashing of the outlaw Bryce will cut his men loose to take over the town. Deb finally finishes carrying the basket I rush her home once entering the house I place the basket on the kitchen counter and go into the bedroom and retrieve my war bag from under the bed I hesitate to open it memories of hot lead, gunsmoke and fear flood over me. I remember the words of a great man he always said, "being brave is being scared as hell but saddling up anyway, I open the bag.

CHAPTER 3

DEATH IN THE STREET

The black smooth leather gun belt feels cool and comfortable in my hand, like meeting an old friend, I strap the gun rig around my waist and tie down the holster resting on my right thigh, I pull the .44 Smith and Wesson Russian six gun from my holster give it the once over and making sure it is fully loaded before returning it to the black holster the weight of the 6 gun gives me a sense of comfort, next I pull the heavy hitting .44 Schofield from my belly holster repeat the process and slide it back into place. Reaching once again into my war bag I pull out my double barrelled sawed down 12 gauge greener break it open sliding 2 big cartridges into the tubes then I snap it shut and put extra shells in my vest pockets, the last item I remove from my bag is a long black bandana real nice material paid dearly for it, I tie it around my neck if I am going to die I am going to look good doing it. Once more I am forced to take lives not by choice but to save and protect the innocents the code demands the return of the Man from Mustang.

Deb stands shocked when I come out of the bedroom loaded for bear, although she fears for me she knows as a man of the west I have to take a stand my beautiful wife is sort of like the gals of old Greece and Sparta. Come back holding your shield or be carried back on it, proud strong amazing woman and I love her dearly. I walk to her and wrap her up in my arms and hold her telling her everything is alright and I am a tough man to kill, to grabbing on to Deb was easy but letting go was damn hard, we share a long tender kiss and before my nerve fails me I leave my house and head to the vacant Marshals office. Coming in the back door I find Tom and Mayor Kline waiting both men eying my hardware with curiosity but say nothing I address the Mayor, "Mayor Kline I want you to swear me in as Marshal and Tom as Deputy all hell is about to break loose going to be hotter than a whore house on nickle night, Bryce and his cutthroats are going to tree this town unless stopped, my giving that asshole Pen a licking is just the excuse they have been waiting for, I have seen this before Mayor and it ain't pretty, now how about those badges."

"Gabe you put me in a hell of a position if I deputize you I am sending you to almost certain death your are outnumbered by desperate killers, that is a tough bunch Bryce has, how about if we try to round up some of the men in town put the numbers on our side run them polecats out on a rail." I am getting real low on patience by now and in a harsher tone then I intended I tell the Mayor, "Mr. Kline there are 2 things wrong with your idea the first it will take to long to round up men ready to fight and second the townsmen are no match for these killer outlaws there will be many funerals. Before my time here I worked with my guns and tamed a couple mining towns I just want Tom covering my back and everyone off the streets make no mistake Mayor their blood will flow." The Mayor having no other dumbass volunteers digs out a couple badges and with about a 30 second swearing in we are now the law in town, I advise the mayor to get word to everyone to get home to their houses and stay away from the windows.

Tom smiles at me, "well Hoss you got what you wanted I sure hope you got a plan I am going to be some riled if I am dead and miss one of Deb's fried chicken dinners", just then the spy brothers come quietly in the back door saying Bryce and his polecats are busting up the saloon lots of loud talk and cursing, I thank the boys and tell them to go right home the fight was coming real soon now. "Ok Tom it is here now like it or not, Pard I need you to find a good spot where you can see the whole street and make sure you have some cover, now I am going to face them in the street they will be cocky and over confident when I let loose with the scattergun you pick off the men on the far left and right I will deal with the assholes standing in front of me now lets get going we need to be ready and waiting good luck Dad." We shake hands just in case then Tom goes seeking a good sniper position I walk outside and stand in the shade where I can see the front of the saloon, as I wait I fire up a thin black cigar its harsh bite calms me, me mouth dry palms wet damn I hate waiting.

I am just about to fire up my second cigar when the saloons batwing door bang open and the outlaws pour out taking a deep breath I step into the middle of the street and call out," Bryce this is the law I am ordering you and your men to surrender your arms and come peaceable to the jail, if you resist arrest I will kill you like the vermin with you- sure as shooting." The outlaws now turn their attention to me and at leader Grimm's orders fan out across the street, the town toughs Clem and Mason were on the ends, Bryce in the centre with Lefty on one side and a sorry looking Pen on the other, as I figured Bryce would be a talker. I see Lefty looking at me like trying to remember who I was, Bryce hooks his thumbs in his belt and with a snake like grin begins his boast, "well looky here boys the law ain't he fearsome looking, law dog after we shoot you to doll rags we are going to rape your sweet wife and burn down this shithole town, "as the outlaw leader talk I keep walking closer to the group of men I need to get into effective scattergun range. "Bryce you boys ain't near tough as you think just ask Lefty's back shooter cousin, I enjoyed putting him under you remember me yet Lefty?" Recognition hits Lefty like a bucket of ice water, "Boss I remember who this son of a bitch is he killed my cousin and many others they call him the Man from Mustang and folks say he is pure grease lighting with his six shooters." The smile leaves Bryce's face and his hand reaches for his colt peacemaker I pull both triggers of the shotgun Pen is almost torn in half and Bryce takes a few pellets in the left shoulder, I hear Tom's rifle cough and see Mason go down, I drop the shotgun before it hits the ground I have my .44 out bucking in my hand Lefty's chest is torn apart as 2 large chunks of hot lead smash through bones and shred organs, then like getting kicked by a horse my leg goes out a bullet smashing my shin. Bryce is the only outlaw left standing but bleeding out from at least 3 holes in him he lifts his gun up for a kill shot but my .44 slug through his eye left him coming up short, as sudden as it started it is over, the only sound is my heavy breathing and the ringing in my ears.

Tom comes walking back down the street I am happy to see him not hurt, Deb would have my hide, damn good man to have your back, people are slowly coming out of their shelters reminding me of gophers, the brothers are escorting the doctor and my lovely wife to where I am now sitting in the street having a cigar and thinking how good a coffee would be right about now. Deb holds on to me tight as the saw bones looks over my injured leg and tells me I am lucky it is a clean break and I should be up and moving around in a couple weeks. I take off my badge and study it for a few seconds before handing it to Tom, "give these back to the Mayor Dad jobs done."

BE SURE YOUR FEET ARE IN THE RIGHT PLACE, THEN STAND FIRM- ABRAHAM LINCOLN

STORY 9

BE TOUGH BUT FAIR

CHAPTER 1

THE SGT MAJOR

Damn it is hot and dryer than a hard morning after, makes me yearn for my Blue mountains with streams the water so cold it hurts your teeth I recon I should introduce myself I am Cpl Piper Hennessy and am currently riding with the US 6th Cavalry Regiment. Currently I am hunting blood thirty Apache warriors in Hells frying pan Arizona but I thank the war gods I am riding with Sgt Major Oskar Kozaczuk best damn NCO in the regiment a real hardass but he looks after his men and we know it. As you can probably tell from the name the Sgt Major he ain't from around here he was born and raised in Poland his father a famous Army General and Politician, when of age Oskar the legendary 15th Uhlans Regiment and his ancestors can be traced back to rider warriors with the nations pride the Winged Hussars. Oskar proved himself a natural leader with a sharp military mind combined with his cool courage under fire got himself promoted to Major at a young age and was a rising star destined for great things until the fateful day he met the Baroness she was renowned for her beauty and affairs in which left a string of broken or dead men by their own hand.

I recon old Oskar was a striking figure in his fancy officer uniform, he stands 6 foot 1 in his socks, wide across the shoulder and chest narrow hips and just a touch bowlegged, deep piercing blue eyes with blonde hair and moustache, a man who women wanted and men wanted to be. He stands tall, straight and with the proper military bearing, as I hear it did not take long for the Baroness bitch to put him under her spell and that would not have been to bad but another man claims the lady's attention a man of wealth and power. Arrogant to a fault thought himself a duelist as 2 men have died by his gun, after some verbal jousting the man foolishly challenges the Major to a duel, Oskar hoping not to kill his opponent chose sabre's hoping to wound or unarm him. It really did not matter what weapons were used the Major was skilled in about any weapon used to kill other men or animals and had no problem getting his hands dirty with some knuckle and skull. The seconds and judge for the duel were agreed upon and it was decided the duel would take place in a isolated park just outside city limits at sunrise the next morning, Oskar did not want this fight but to withdraw not would be a sign of weakness and cowardness and the Sgt Major ain't neither.

Dew lays heavy on the grass and the morning sun is burning off a light ground fog when the men go to work with their sharp cold steel, from the start everyone present can see that Oskar was the superior fighter and could end it at any time but he wanted to teach his opponent a painful lesson. Within minutes the man is bleeding from no less than 6 minor cuts and bruised from where the Major slapped his man with the flat of his sword. The Major had had enough and gives his opponent the chance to escape with his life and most of his pride, enraged the man charges swing his sabre wildly Oskar has not choice but run the crazed man through, the mans eyes glaze over and fade hanging off the Major's sword, Oskar pulls his sword from the mans body he is already dead when he crashes face first into the cool wet grass.

Well I will tell you what Oskar paid dearly for the killing both the Royalty and the High Command were unhappy about the duel and made a public example of the Major he was given a choice of prison or resigning his Commission and leaving Poland immediately, Oskar being no dummy handed in his uniform and sword and got the first ship to the Americas. Arriving in New York during the 3rd year of the civil war within days of being on American soil was made Sgt in the Iron Brigade. When the insanity and the cannons stopped ending the war Oskar was a Captain at wars end, Oskar is unsure of his future until he hears the Cavalry is looking for men to fight the wild Indians of the west liking the thought of seeing some wild country and the adventure. Oscar signs on with the fighting 6th Cavalry and is now top soldier and experienced Indian fighter. The Sgt Major and myself met in the last year of the war and when he signs up to go Indian fighting, I figure what the hell and sign the dotted line, I can be a dumbass.

CHAPTER 2

DON'T DO THE CRIME IF YOU CANNOT DO THE TIME

Home at present for the Sgt Major and myself is Fort Bowie in south eastern Arizona, a lovely spot with boiling hot desert heat, deep canyons, volcanic rock and mountain ranges and if it is good year it may even rain twice a year. It is a perfect place for Apache hunting, and I mean them hunting us, them warriors are a tough breed and deadly. The Apache are guerrilla fighters and master of the ambush, since arriving at Fort Bowie we have played taps for 9 of our fallen brothers almost to a man the troopers fear being taken alive by the Apache who among other things are masters of is torture can keep a man alive for days before letting them die. I have had young Troopers ask me the best way to kill themselves, my answer is always eat the bullet, or knife in the throat or eye. Today we are in garrison and I am duty Cpl and with an unneeded guard I am escorting Sgt's Reilly and Flanagan along with a young Trooper from Tennessee named York, what a sorry looking bunch all look rode hard and put away wet, seems the Sgt's discovered Trooper York's still hidden in some heavy brush just outside the fort and being first rate NCO,s cannot accuse the trooper without making sure it is moonshine he is making is real hootch, they proceed to test enough of it to sink a battle ship. They were arrested while singing arm and arm old Irish songs and taken to the brig to await the wrath of the Sgt Major one of the Troopers on guard duty placed a pail of fresh water in the cell knowing the boys were going to wake up with serious case of cotton mouth. We now reach the Headquarters office and the prisoners are at attention waiting to be called into the Sgt Majors office not a good way to start your morning.

I know Oskar is making them wait and sweat it out a bit finally I hear him command, "Cpl Hennessey march the guilty bastards in." I call out double time and bring them to a halt in front of Oskar's desk I leave them at attention sitting he looks up eyeballing each man then abruptly comes to his feet his blond completion now showing some red with anger. Now Sgt's Reilly and Flanagan have been together with us through some hard times and tough scraps, all saving each others lives more than once and fighting shoulder to shoulder but that ain't going to get them out of this pickle. In an angry loud tone the Sgt Major breaks the silence damn even after all these years I jump, "Sgt's Reilly and Flanagan your are busted down to Cpl I would bust you to shit shoveling Trooper but I need NCO'S even if it is you 2 dumbasses. We have a war on but for the next while every dirty dangerous job is coming your way, you will continue your duties but report the guardhouse directly after supper you will be sleeping there for the next 2 weeks, now for you Trooper York I had your still destroyed but I had the men save me a sample I remember another Tennessee boy in the Iron Brigade who made some fine bust skull whiskey name of Samuel York your Grandfather I believe. Building a still is serious offence but your actions last night will be forgiven due to a couple ex Sgt's being of bad influence. The Sgt Major then reaches into his desk and pulls a quart bottle of Trooper York's white lightning, he takes his time knowing the suffering of the hungover men. Licking his lips he takes a long pull off the bottle taking the bottle from his lips he whistles and blows his breath out, damn Trooper York you are an artist, this may even be better than your Grandaddies, Trooper York you will spend 2 weeks in the stockade and will have stable duty every day plus 2 hours of sentry duty until released, now do you men accept my punishment or is it a court martial you want?"

Without hesitation the 3 guilty men accepted their assigned punishment after the charges were finished he put the men at ease and let each man have a big drink of home brew, he told me I could indulge I take a healthy swallow coughing I hand the bottle back to Oskar he takes one last drink and pours the rest out the open window, "Cpl Hennessy march the guilty bastards out, dismissed." Once out of the office all concerned breathed a sigh of relief that event is over the Sgt Major is a commanding figure and just one scary damn soldier, I have Trooper York escorted to the stables and the new Cpls to carry on with there duties, I am off to the chow hall I am in serious need of a coffee. The Sgt Major runs a tight ship and is a disciplinarian keeps it pretty simple reward and punishment, follow the rules you will never have a problem with him but get out of line and you will feel his wrath, in garrison he is everywhere keeping an eye on things. He always takes time to talk with the men especially the young troopers Oskar knows every mans first name under his command. By damn it is fun to watch the old boy go after some young Trooper his voice loud with that heavy Polish accent damn fun if you are not the one under his gaze. Overall most of the Troops like him but more important like him or not they respect him and in any military respect is hard earned and is to most more important than life itself. The Sgt Major is hard and does push the men hard but no harder than himself he knows weak men die easy in Apache country, he feels it is his duty to do everything to keep his men alive and motivate them to fight like Viking Beserkers of old.

I do as little as possible for the rest of the day and this evening I am jawing with the new Cpl's through the brig barred windows when we here a commotion coming from behind the stables men's voices raised in excitement, I tell the prisoners we better go check it out they leave their unlocked cell. We 3 Cpl's have fought shoulder to shoulder with Oskar and with survival we have become closer than brothers Reilly and Flanagan are a couple of wild broncs but they would never break a trust to the Sgt Major. We wander over and discover that a couple of Troopers were about to settle a disagreement with fist a cuffs, entertainment is rare in the wilderness so most of the Troop was there watching, it is a soldiers fight so I will not interfere unless things get out of hand I look to the 2 combatants damn this may get ugly. It is going to be a very uneven contest Trooper Smears is a big brute and bully uses his size to intimidate new troops and smaller men, now looks to me like young Trooper Lee is having none of it even though he was 5 inches shorter and 40 pounds lighter than Smears, the kid has guts but I fear he is going to take a beating at the hands of the brute. Sudden silence falls over the group as the Sgt Major walks into the middle of circle of men, he looks to me and my prisoners but says nothing, damn that Oskar don't miss a damn thing showing a frown he looks around the group before speaking I know he has read the signs and needs no explaining, "So it is soldiers fight ya ok I am referee and if I say its over you stop Trooper Lee Trooper Smears do you understand if so get ready?"

Trooper Lee could not be more than 18 years old a proud southern soldier who has a famous relative, but he is still between the straw and the hay and not many scraps under his belt, but he is game. On the other hand Trooper Smears has a long history of fighting mostly men he knew he could beat I suspect him a coward, but in knuckle and skull fighting he is strong, brutal and dangerous. The rules in this sort of fight are if a man is knocked down it is the end of the round and they break until called by the referee if a man cannot get up or make it to the mark he loses, I do not really think you could call it a fight Trooper Lee takes a beating, Smears being the asshole would hold the young trooper up by the collar and keep punching him until Oskar steps in and stops the fight to the great displeasure of Trooper Smears. Then something wonderful happens Smears opens his big mouth, "Sgt Major you had no right to stop the fighting I owe that little smart mouth more but how about you pulling your blouse I figure all this talk on how tough you are is all brag how about it Sgt major want some?" Oskar says nothing but turns and walks over to me and after removing his tunic he hands it to me to hold smiling he rolls up his sleeves and turns to face his opponent, me and the boys are tickled pink this piece of shit is going to get his bell rung.

Both men come up to the mark, Smears throws a hard left hook sucker punch to the side of Oskar's face but the old fighter saw it coming and was able to turn his head enough to avoid the full impact, Oskar does not even take a step back he just smiles and spits out a gob of blood and saliva, Smear goes white knowing he hit the Sgt Major with his best Sunday punch and the man laughed it off. Now Oskar goes to work, and it is a thing of beauty to watch first Oskar gets in close throwing 2 hard jabs then a sweet right cross and a vicious left hook to the body. Then from the hip he throws and uppercut hitting the big man on the point chin Trooper Smears eyes roll back into his head then after swaying for a few seconds falls face first into the hard ground. Cheers go up from the men Reilly and Flanagan laugh and slap Oskar on the back, the Sgt Major then calls Trooper Lee over, "Let's take a look at you Chlopak, (his term for young green troops) you fought a good fight ya, it is not always about winning or losing but how you handle yourself, now lets see that eye looks like a deep cut, Cpl Hennessy will take you to the sawbones get a few stitches. You will have nice scar to lie about to young ladies ya, you 2 prisoners back to the guardhouse on the double, back to your barracks all of you and stay there, dismissed."

The next morning the duty Cpl finds me at chow he tells me the Sgt Major wants to see me on the double that can only mean only one thing we be riding and about time I will take Apaches and the wilderness over garrison boredom any day. Smiling to myself now looking forward to some action I take a last gulp of coffee then with a brisk jaunty step I head over to the HQ's, see what fun the Sgt Major has volunteered me for now.

CHAPTER 3

THE PATROL

I no sooner get through in the door when Oskar ushers me into the Commanding Officers office, now I know for sure we are going out suddenly I have an unexplained sense of dread but it only lasts a few seconds I shake it off and wait for the orders. Waiting along with the Commander is a young shave tail Lt. named Lucas Hood only 4 months out of West point academy and his first assignment I think he will make a fine officer if we can keep him alive long enough to learn. He has warrior blood running through his veins his great Uncle was General Hood a famous Confederate general and warrior. The Commander quickly gets to the briefing Lt. Hood with 2 NCO's and 10 men with proceed to the Turkey Creek stage station with all haste word has come that the passengers are trapped inside the station building they are surrounded but the station is built like a fort with rock walls they may still be alive. "Lt. Hood I am sending Cpl Hennessy with you as scout as you know at the moment we have no Apache scouts but Hennessy here is a good as any Apache man can track a skeeter through a rain storm. Now gentlemen you know your duty expedite, time is critical, word has it there is a woman and child at the besieged station pray you get there first, if no questions dismissed."

Once out of the Commanders office the Lt. tells me I am to hand pick the troopers he wants only men with fighting experience on this patrol, damn smart move, and be in the saddle in 30 minutes and he was off and running. Just as I was exiting the Sgt Major informs me he will be going out with us and have old Iron Head saddled Oskar has to be due to his rank a good garrison soldier but he like me would rather be in the hurricane deck going out looking for a fight. He of course will not inform the Commander top soldiers are not supposed to go out on patrols but that did not sit well with Oskar. He never liked other men doing his fighting for him and it keeps him battle ready things can happen right quick out in the sand and cactus, but the Old Man is going to pop a blood vessel when he finds out, Oskar knew he would pay a price but as a Sgt Major and Medal of Honour winner and is pretty much fire proof.

Reilly and Flanagan are beside themselves that I cannot let them come along but with Oskar with the patrol there was no way, they tell me to keep my ass down when the arrows fill the air and take care of Oskar, those boys surely do miss a good scrap. I go hunt up Trooper York I know that Tennessee moonshiner is also a right fine tracker and fighter, all the other men chosen were battle hardened veterans who all at one time fought with or against Oskar and myself. This is a tough wang leather bunch the Sgt Major looks over the men and nods his agreement until he sees Trooper York, "Sgt Major Trooper York here is a good scout and can read sign I can use him there is some real tough country we have to get through." Oskar smiles and gives me a pat on the back, 40 minutes after leaving the Commanders officer with the Lt and Sgt Major in the lead we thunder through the wide gates of the fort we will push hard for a couple hours then give the horses a breather. The men all know to take care of their horses even if it means going without giving his animal the last of his water, a man out here on foot will give the coyotes and crows a nice meal, there is little hope of survival.

Lt Hood orders the scouts forward Trooper York and myself move out about a ¼ mile in front of the patrol but always where we can be seen, the tough part about scouting is you have to look down for tracks and other sign while some villain is up in the rocks with his front sight on you. The feeling of being exposed or as we say alone and at the end of the branch will test the mettle of the bravest of men and I sure ain't near the bravest but I do the best I can with what I have. Everything seems quiet not sure if I like this or not Trooper York waves to catch my attention and signals me to join him, by the time I ride over to him he is off his horse and looking close at the marks on the ground I have a good look around before climbing down joining the young Trooper, does not take more than a glance to see his concern at least 10 unshod horses passed this way no more than a couple hours ago I take off my hat and way it to the troop telling them to move forward to our position. The tracks read as plain as day they were heading the same direction we are towards the Fowler ranch I recon joining others there, that could mean the Fowler family are still alive I know the rancher has a couple tough as nails fighters riding for him. The Lt. is from Texas and needs no explanation he knows we are in a tough spot we know we have warriors in front and I recon more closing in from behind and all heading for the Fowler ranch no doubt in my dull mind it's going to get hotter than a whorehouse on nickle night.

The Lt and Sgt Major take a couple minutes to discuss how to proceed and rightly agree we need speed over caution unless we come across a possible ambush site there will be no flankers out we will push the horses and ourselves hard to the very limit if we are going to help the people at the ranch. The Lt knows Oskar is the most experienced horseman and lets him set the pace through experience and a sharp mind the Sgt Major knows just how far he can push if you push to hard the result is dead men and horses, There must still be enough grit left in them for the fight. For the next 2 hours Oskar sets a killing pace the landscape is just a blur I am totally focused on the wild ride trying to keep pace urging the men on just when I think Oskar has sunstroke and lost his mind he pulls off into a shady spot under a low cliff to give men and mostly the horses a rest.

The Sgt Major then orders every man to wash out the dust from their horses nostrils and give our mounts as much water as we can we are close now so we are also to check our weapons our spencer rifles will be in hand from here on in, even the break feels like we were moving in high gear, I can now sense the tension in the men getting themselves ready for a battle and making peace with their gods-just in case.

The Sgt Major barks at me to get the troops mounted have carbines drawn and ready again the Sgt Major sets a horse killing pace suddenly we can hear rifle shots music to my ears this means there are still people alive and fighting. Then I watch in horror and as in slow motion I see Trooper York's horse get its front foot caught in a gopher hole and goes down the young Trooper has no time to escape and the horse falls on him both horse and man do not rise. I pull up quick and get to the young Trooper as fast as I can he is in bad shape his left arm and leg broken just for a start and has a nasty cut on his scalp from hitting his head on a small rock, the horse cannot be saved I know I cannot risk a shot so I take out my Arkansas Toothpick and cut the suffering animals throat. The Lt has halted the patrol he and Oskar walk over to the downed soldier there is no time for but just laying it out hard and fast and the Sgt Major does just that, "Trooper it is just bad luck ya, but you know we cannot wait on you are a soldier and like the rest of us take a soldiers chance we will leave you a canteen and a spare pistol and be back to help you as soon as we can, now we must go Chlopak, remember who you are and what outfit you ride for good luck." I walk over to one of the supply mules and pull a sawed off 12 gauge double barrelled shotgun out then stuff my pockets with shells of big buckshot I tell Oskar that I will be staying with the Trooper I am pretty good with injuries and with no cover the Apache would make sport in killing him. If it were any other man but me the Sgt Major may have refused but he knows me to be one stubborn SOB and care little for the backlash, there is just right and wrong. It is a bad spot and we both know it, but he nods his agreement we quickly shake hands just in case and then I am eating their dust off as they bravely ride into battle.

CHAPTER 4

SAVAGE AS A MEAT AXE

Alone now with the injured man I now kneel and give the broken boy the once over, I know he is in extreme pain but is standing up to it like a soldier they grow them tough in Tennessee first thing I do is take out his army colt .45 from its flapped holster and place it by his right hand. We are in open ground no cover but the troopers dead horse, out in the open we will surely be spotted and thinking us for a couple easy scalps warriors will surely be coming for our hair. The shotgun I place beside me then begin a quick examination of the injured Trooper, by the awkward positioning of his left arm and leg it is clear they are both broke and the bones need to be reset and put back in place but I have nothing for splints. I straighten out his body gentle as I the young Trooper goes white with pain, I do not know should I set the breaks now and splint later or wait never a damn medic around when you need one.

They come out of the ground like ghosts I see the Troopers eyes get big as he snatches up his revolver I have no time to look 3 determined looking bad ass warriors are almost upon me when I snatch up the shotgun and let go with both barrels shooting from the hip, I drop the empty shotgun and pull my six shooter from my belt, Trooper York's smokewagon is barking, one Apache is near tore in half by the big hunks of hot buckshot and another wounded but still in the fight, I snap 2 quick shots at him before the 3rd enemy trys to drive his knife into my throat. The barrel of my revolver is in his stomach I pull the trigger and cringe as the hammer hits a bad shell and the revolver fails to fire, to hell with this with a huge heave I throw the Apache off me and as I get to my feet drawing my Arkansas toothpick, I smile now the warrior blood off my ancients pounding through my veins, come get some Hoss lets see who is the better man today. The damn Hennessy luck holds the man across from me is an experienced warrior and is in his element fighting with cold steel, he is good cuts me twice before I get into the fight proper, he feints a stab I do not bite this time but take a quick step right and swing my blade low under his arm the razor sharp steel bites his flesh leaving a long deep cut along his ribs. My enemy has a look of surprise as he touches the wound the blood flows freely soon his hand is covered he then rubs the warm sticky liquid all over his face taking on a fearsome appearance then attacks. Damn he is good and damn fast I better figure a way to end this quick or I may be buzzard bait, just then he over extends a thrust I then tag him with a lovely left hook stunning him long enough for me to drive the huge blade deep into the mans guts, I pull the gory blade out quickly and make a final slash at his throat it cuts like a hot knife through butter I damn near take his head clear off, with sadness I salute a true warrior it was a rare honour to fight such a man.

That Trooper York is one hell of a fighter he killed both warriors coming up from behind me shot them to doll rags I got lucky and killed the buckshot wounded warrior one of my shots goes in just under his eye leaving a large part of his skull missing. The firing has stopped at the ranch my ears are ringing and my eyes are stinging from the acid like gun smoke the silence is deafening it makes me feel nervous and anxious. I watch now as 2 Apache fighters on horse back are high tailing it 3 ways from Sunday away from the I hold my breath hoping they will just keep riding but once we were spotted they change direction and charge. They ride hell for leather right at us and keeping low to the horses back to make them more difficult to shoot them off their horses. Instinct and training now take over I pick up the 12 gauge break it open remove the spent shells and put 2 shells of destruction in the big bores, as much as I hate to do it I know I have to take down their horses they are getting close now I can hear their battle screams. I throw the shotgun to my shoulder and fire the right barrel into the chest of the one spotted pony then cut lose with the left barrel, both horses go down hard. Out of the dust 2 ghost like figures rush towards me one has a old revolver the other a bow and arrow I drop the empty shotgun and draw my army colt.45, holding the trigger down I fan the hammer with the palm of my left hand within a heartbeat I empty my six gun into them the big chucks of hot lead tearing them up and ripping out their souls both now motionless never to rise again.

Quickly I reload both revolvers and the shotgun hoping the fighting is done I smile as I hear the bugler sounding recall and see some of the troop coming back to help us of course the Sgt major is in the lead. He will not show it but knowing him as I do he is beside himself with worry about myself and Trooper York secretly I refer to him at times as Bubba Oskar but I will tell you what there is no man I would rather ride with, best damn man in the Regiment. Thankfully Cpl Miller the Medic is with him I leave Trooper York in his capable hands and after lighting a black cigar I join the Sgt Major he is rubbing his head looking at the 7 dead Apache warriors that lay all around us. The old warrior does not need to be told what happened the story lay in the battlefield but I make sure to tell him of Trooper York's courage and sand in dropping his 2 men, I tell him it was an outstanding display of courage and grit shown by the severely injured man. The big man finally smiles knowing all is well with us and we have survived, "Is good to see you still kicking old friend ya, you boys have a hell of a fight here them Indians learned the hard way what happens when you fight a Wildman from the Blue Mountains and a Tennessee moonshiner ya, the Apache have cleared out and are headed back into the hills but we killed 14 and captured Mango and Jon Jon 2 sub war chiefs. Our losses are light but we have 4 wounded and no one killed a very good day my friend ya." We stand together smoking our cigars in silence watching the medic and a couple men tending to Trooper York's injuries and making a make shift travois to drag him on it will be brutal and painful journey back to the fort but the Troopers injuries are to severe to sit a horse.

A short while later a dispatch rider from the Lt tells the Sgt Major we are going to camp on the Fowler ranch tonight to rest the horses and men, this is good news to me I know they got a nice deep well with good sweet water so cold it hurts your teeth and I am thirstier than a preacher after a 3 day drunk, York is placed as gently as possible on the litter and we lead the men back to the ranch. Riding back I am overwhelmed with weariness and fatigue the intense fire of my warrior blood has cooled it is a familiar but unpleasant feeling of what comes surviving a battle but I know this will pass it is all just part of being a soldier. The first thing I do when we get to the ranch is stick my face full in the water bucket, a cold pleasant sensation immediately flows through my body damn that feels right good, Trooper York is placed under the shade of an ancient live oak tree and seems to be a bit more comfortable he gives me a forced smile, I give him a thumbs up. Supper turns out to be a grand surprise Mr. Fowler showing his thanks brings out to the Troop a smoked ham the size of a buffalo calf, and loaves of fresh bread, you have to give western women respect here she is in the middle of an Indian battle and makes bread for the men, hell of a woman, and ham is a rare treat. Not many people keep pigs because for some unknown reason the Apache have taken a dislike to the animal and they like putting lots of arrows into them. We take our knives and slice up the ham to make huge sandwiches, damn fine chow, I wash it down with some horse shoe floating trail coffee and I am one happy man, lighting up one of my last cigars I look over at my friend Oskar and think of Reilly and Flanagan back at the post and how pissed they are going to be having missed the fun but that was really the Sgt Majors intended punishment, Tough but fair.

THE ULTIMATE MEASURE OF A MAN IS NOT WHERE HE STANDS IN MOMENTS OF COMFORT BUT WHERE HE STANDS IN TIMES OF CHALLENGE- MARTIN LUTHER KING JR

STORY 10

DO WHAT HAS TO BE DONE

CHAPTER 1

SCRAPER AND THE DEUCE

Sam Scraper Carson and Bruce The Deuce Bass are sitting on a couple rickety wooden chairs and using a short wooden barrel as a table in which they are playing checkers just a few feet from the batwing doors of the Red Ruby saloon both men now in their 60's and in their youth hell on wheels holy terrors in any type of fight. Scraper and Deuce met as young men during the Civil War riding for the famous Confederate General Ashby the unit was known as the Black Knights of the Confederacy and through luck teamwork and skill they both managed to survive 11 major engagements, both men sport scars of wounds suffered during the bloody conflict. After the wars end the two men as soldiers do have become closer than brothers and decide it might be fun to join the Yankee Cavalry and go fight wild Indians, well they got their wish and more from White mountain Apaches, Utes and the Paiutes of southern Arizona, fighting was hot, dirty, dangerous and very bloody on both sides, often with desperate men fighting hand to hand with cold steel.

Both men for their bravery and fighting skills were Sgt's when their hitch was up but decided they have had enough fun time to try something new. With gold and silver mines opening all over the west their was a need for lawman not peace officers but iron on iron hard town tamers and bounty hunters, they say outlaws and night riders black hearts filled with fear if they heard Scraper and the Deuce were on their backtrail, they were like bulldogs never letting go would follow a man into the 6th layer of hell and pump lead into the devil himself to get their men.

Now living in Kingsman Arizona the 2 men spend their time smoking drinking coffee and playing checkers or crib, there is quite a contrast in the men, Scraper is fairly tall about 6 foot 1 slim with the wide shoulders of a riders his hair is now silver he keeps it long like Hickok is right proud of that big handlebar moustache under his nose, very even tempered speaks little but with old habits dying hard is always on the watch for trouble. Now The Deuce is a way different critter about 5 foot 10, huge upper body with thick arms that stretch the mans shirt, short thick legs hands the size of hams and scarred from countless battles, the Deuce loves a good scrap, he always wears a beat up brown derby and under the derby is a head as bald a billiard ball which in the sun shines brightly. The Deuce loves to hear himself talk and is a bit of a motor mouth he is constantly jabbering about something or other, but for all their differences they hold a tight bond few men get the privilege to enjoy.

The morning is like most mornings in Arizona warm, calm and sunny, Scraper and Deuce had not began the games yet just enjoying the beautiful morning with coffee and cigars, both men sit quiet enjoying the peace and quiet of the morning, the men's heads turn when they hear horses riding down the street figuring it was some cowboys come to town for supplies and a few drinks. It is not cowboys but a rough outlaw bunch Slasher Flint Moon and his 4 killer horsemen. Slasher and his mob are well known in Arizona, Texas and even old Mexico. This bunch gives outlaws a bad name they enjoy the killing more than the robberies cruel bloodthirsty and not above the most devastating crimes, Rape, pretending not to notice the approaching riders the 2 old men concentrate on the game, nothing is going to happen yet. Earlier that morning the widow Nora Summers stopped by on her way to her dress shop and brought the boys some homemade oatmeal cookies a big stack on one of her china plates, she told to boys to enjoy and it would be nice if Bruce would return the plate this evening, the Widow Summers has her sights dead set on the Deuce as her next husband, poor man does not know he is done for yet.

Deuce laughs and points to the far end of the street seems Marshal Hickley has heard of the new guests in town and has urgent and pressing business anywhere but the town of Kingsman, nice fella the Marshal got himself a bit of a yellow streak a mile wide. The 5 hard trail weary and dirty men dismount tie their horses to the hitching rack and head for the saloon Scraper and Deuce ignore them. One of the outlaws stops in front of the men, he is known as Tombstone Boucher and he had trouble written all over him, all he sees is 2 useless old men past their prime.

CHAPTER 2

DUSTING OFF THE 6 GUNS

Tombstone was a brute of a man bully, intimidator and just plain rattlesnake mean, standing in front of the 2 checker players he starts digging in his spurs calling them worthless old codgers who should just walk out into the desert and disappear, Scraper and Deuce continue to ignore the beast. Old Tombstone does not like the way he is being treated so be knocks over the checkerboard and breaks Nora's nice China plate. Deuce livid comes to his feet quick but before he can get set Boucher sucker punches him sending the big man staggering back then grabs on to a post so not to fall, after a few seconds Deuce lifts his head and smiles at Tombstone. He turns head and spits out a huge glob of blood and saliva, the scene goes dead quiet as the unmistakable sound of shotgun hammers being pulled back is heard. Slasher and his men now see Scraper holding rock steady a 12 gauge double barrel greener shotgun, there is no mistake his look, his gray eyes hard no other expression, Slasher and his men know they were looking at death this tall old man would kill them dead-sure as shooting. Scraper then points the shotgun at Tombstone, "Undo and drop your gunbelt then walk out into the street you are looking for a fight and my Pard here is going to oblige you took your shot and did not even knock him off his feet my old granny could hit harder, now the rest of you any man interferes or touches a gun will be cut in half, now that work for you Bruce?"

Deuce as Sam expected was raring to go spitting into his huge hands he then rubs they together and walks out waiting for the brute to meet him, Boucher laughs and kids with his with his bunch telling them to watch as he breaks the old mans back. The 2 fighters now stand in front of each other Boucher towering over the Deuce cursing the shorter man out telling how he is to punish the old man, deuce just smiles says nothing then backhands the big man who staggers back in pain and surprise, "now you piece of shit why not try to throw that big punch again." Well damned is exactly what the dumbass did he throws a powerful swing left hook at the Deuce's head, the old battler seen it coming from a mile away and goes under the swing, Boucher now has left himself open and Deuce makes him pay, Bruce lets go a vicious left hook to Boucher's ribs men cringe at the sound of the live bone breaking, Tombstone screams and begins to double over Deuce then follows the hook with tremendous right hand to the big mans jaw just under his left ear, Tombstones eyes roll back in his head and falls face first into the hard street breaking his nose. Sam then tells Slasher to get his man off the street and go have a few drinks they behave themselves there will be no more trouble, and it will cost them 5 dollars to replace the Widow summers good china plate. Slasher pays up but is not pleased, but get out of line now will mean barking guns, Sam holds the shotgun on the outlaws until they are in the bar then gently puts the hammers back down. Sam tells Bruce they got to go to the general store and get Nora a new plate and then they would go over the Roughrider Café for lunch.

The 5 dollars they got from Slasher should buy a much nicer plate than the one broken of course Deuce wanted to grab one and leave and get chow but Sam told him they need to get Miss Nora something nice to show off to the ladies when they have their hen parties. Well I recon it is time to let you in on a little secret Nora has a partner in crime in the capturing the reluctant courter, and of course that would be Sam. The men find what they hope is the perfect plate it is oval, of good English china decorated with bluebells and blue birds all around the outside rim of the dish, Sam tells Bruce he will finish up and get the plate wrapped but he is low on cigars and asks him pick up 20 or so,that will have him at the other end of the store. Sam calls over the owner a old trail hand who had enough sleeping on the ground and asks him to wrap up the dish real pretty and he needs a card and pencil for a note, everyone in town knew what was going on but poor Deuce the owner smiles and winks gathering up the articles. Neither Sam or Bruce had much school learning both had a hard hand with a pen so Nora will not suspect Sam writing the note after a minutes thought smiling Sam begins writing- "Miss Nora some villian's broke your cookie dish, me and Sam collected money from them and bought you a new dish we hope you take to it, much obliged for the cookies. If I am not to forward maybe we can have supper one evening soon, your servant Bruce." Just before leaving Sam buys a couple boxes of .44 shells and a box of 12 gauge buckshot shells, Bruce does the same, leaving the store they head to the small house or big shack whichever way you look at it they know whats coming and they know what must be done for there is none else to protect the townspeople, time to dust off and oil the killing tools.

Having worked enforcing law or something close to it they knew the pattern, the men would eat,drink and enjoy the soiled doves tonight but tomorrow they will be hungover mean and broke. They will then take what they want by guns and force they will kill without mercy and take what they want including women, Dapper Dan Tate one of Slashers polecats is a known rapist and woman killer. The 2 men sit quiet at the table they take great care in breaking their guns down cleaning and slightly oiling the weapons. To Scraper and the Deuce a gun was no different from a from any other tool and like any good tradesman you take care of your tools and they will take care of you, finished the men head to the café for supper. Sam still carrying the greener and Deuce now has a huge dragoon army colt revolver stuck in his belt for a quick grab if need be.

Slasher sits grimly looking deep into his shot of red eye thinking about how close they were to getting caught by that damn Arizona Ranger, Regret Cooper who is now known through out the west as the Stormrider one of the toughest lawmen in all Arizona. If it were not for the freak thunderstorm wiping out their tracks and giving them their chance to escape, they would be under the flowers or jail by now. The outlaw boss is under no illusions that the Ranger is still on the trail, there no damn give in the man, Tombstone is coming around slowly damn that was something how that old man put him down. Cursing he knows there is something familiar about these old timers but his memory fails him but his coyote instincts these men cannot be taken lightly and he would make sure they die first. Tombstone comes awake confused madder than a wet hen threatening death, Slasher tells him to pull in his horns they will handle the old men tomorrow gut shoot them and watch them die slow, from a darkened corner comes a loud chuckle. "You boys sure do think a heap of yourselves, you are all lucky to be alive them 2 men have fought everything but the bottle and survived killed more man than the plague on your best day none of you come as high as their boot tops and in case you still have not figured it out they were once known and feared folks used to call them Scratcher and the Deuce". The mystery man chuckles again Slasher livid moves towards the speakers table but comes up short, the man is huge a mountain of a mountain man, dressed in beautiful buckskin. On the table a no nonsense hogleg looking big enough to have wheels, slasher knew bad odds when he saw them turning he heads back to his table once again the big mountain man chuckles. Despite the passing years Scratcher and the Deuce were still well known though tales of their exploits in saloons and around campfires, with the Stormrider on their backtrail and 2 deadly men waiting outside Slasher feels a chill and feels that the walls are closing in on him there may be no escape this time but one thing damn sure he ain't going to prison escape or death no third option.

Supper finished Sam suggests to Bruce that it would be a good time to take the plate to Nora if he is lucky might get invited in for tea and cookies, to his satisfaction Sam received one of Bruce's hard looks and says they both should go she brought cookies for the both of him, smiling again Sam reminds his Amigo that Miss Nora especially asked for him and Sam is not invited. Now you would think The Deuce was walking the 13 steps it is utterly amazing the effect one little gal can have on a man, here is a man who has charged against overwhelming odds, proven his bravery many times over now terrified of speaking to Nora, Bruce never had the knack with women like Sam had they always made him edgy and ill at ease. Slowly he stands and picking up the wrapped gift and walking about as slow as a man can once out the door Sam, Cookie and a couple locals let out a good laugh, Bruce hears it and cringes, but the hell of it is he is smitten with Nora and adores her, smiling now he is confident he will have the last hee haw. Bruce takes a few seconds to straighten out his clothing and removes his derby before gently knocking on the door his heart beat increases as he hears Nora coming to the door, damn women, Nora opens the door and welcomes him in, the soft light of the room gives this beautiful woman a radiance almost that of an earth angel.

Well seems Sam is right again Bruce is invited to tea but instead of cookies Nora has baked a chocolate cake, now this something really special in the wilds of Arizona ingredients are hard to find, a rare treat, stomach wins over brain next thing the big man is sitting at the kitchen table trying to figure how to hold his tiny teacup in his huge paw. Nora has mercy on him and brings him a coffee mug, Bruce then gives her the gift and says for her to open it up. Nora with girlish excitement slowly unwraps the present and lets out a gasp of pleasure and surprise when he sees the serving plate, then she sees the card now how the hell did that get there. Sure as shooting this is Sam's handiwork, Nora opens the card and to Bruce's further discomfort reads it aloud, damn that Sam, then before he knows it Nora up and gives him a big hug, the big mans heart sings. Nora then with true women logic chastises him for putting himself in danger for 50 cent plate, and she heard about the scrap he was in and mentioned something about being to old for rough housing, but she is very pleased with her new platter and he is to thank Sam the ladies will all envy her now when having tea.

Bruce cannot remember a more lovely and peaceful evening the lovers talk is low soft and sweet and before he knows it two hours have passed, reluctantly he tells Nora he must go but he appreciated the cake and her kindness. He does not mention anything about the fight sure to come tomorrow but with a voice sterner than he intended he tell. her she must not go out until he comes back to tell her it is safe. Nora smiles because she knows it is out of concern and love he speaks to her in this way. There are no secrets in small towns Nora knows of the dangers that her Man and Sam would face tomorrow, before Bruce leaves the two lovers embrace in a long hug Bruce holding her tender in his huge arms enjoying the smell of her freshly washed hair, before they separate she lets him. "You be real tough out there tomorrow wang leather tough those men are pure evil and you boys don't move as fast anymore, tell Sam I will be thinking of you both now get out you big pug before I start blubbering", with that she kisses him on the cheek and rushes back to the kitchen. Gently closing the front door behind him Deuce heads back to the shack by instinct and training keeping to the shadows but now thinking to himself how the hell did that happen.

CHAPTER 3

THE TAKEDOWN AND A WEDDING

Sam is still up smoking one of his thin black Mexican cigars and drinking some reheated Arbuckle's, Bruce pours himself a cup and joins his old Amigo at the table, "Pretty slick trick slipping that note in for Nora to read she thinks I wrote the damn thing best not forget Hoss payback is a bitch, now what's our plan for dealing with Slasher and his mob. I got to tell you Pard they trouble me there are no boundaries in their evil black hearts I recon we must put them down quick permanent like." Sam smiles at his at his grumpy friend, "Hoss I have been thinking on it and as I see it there are 2 ways to go we can hit them fast and hard shoot them down like the rabid skunks they are or we can take them alive let the Ranger have em. We will be giving the Territory a first rate hanging affair lot's of folks want to see Slasher and his men hang, see it and know he is gone for good. "This evening while you were courting I went to se Doc Henry the saw bones and after explaining things to him he gives me this, "Sam holds up a small vile of clear liquid his smile growing," now it is time to man up and make the sacrifice Bruce I need one of the bottles of bonded Irish whiskey you got hidden under your bunk, we will get the bartender to give the spiked bottle to them and take them while they are knocked out, what say you Amigo."

Bruce mouth open and stares at his friend as though he has lost his flipping mind, the thought of giving his fine whisky has him in a bit of shock and asks Sam if they just cannot shoot them. Sam tells him they will do it his way Bruce's future bride the lovely Nora would probably frown on them ruthlessly shooting down and eliminating Slasher and the gang. Cursing the whole time, the Deuce goes and retrieves a bottle growling like wounded grizzly, Sam calms him telling him they must have a couple drinks from the bottle before they put in the knockout drops. Bruce gets a couple glasses while Sam opens the bottle, it smells like peat and Ireland, Sam to pacify his Amigo pours the big man a near full glass from him and Sam has a small one, they drink to each others health and to the chaos they hope to bring to the outlaw's world. Drinks finished the 2 men head to the saloon they would go in the back door and try to get Knuckles the bartenders attention to slip him the doctored bottle, the boys have known Knuckles a long while back when the now bartender was a boxing prize fighter. He is a man who cares about the town and its people and will not hesitate to help. Luck is with the boys the back door is unlocked and they slip into the dark storeroom unseen, they can hear Slasher and the gang loud and half drunk boasting and bragging it up, Knuckles is behind the bar back to them, the Deuce picks up a small piece of coal and aiming at the mans back but throwing coal is not one of his skills and hits Knuckles behind the mans left ear with more force then he intended. Knuckles jumps and curses luckily no one notices he glares towards the back room flexing his big scarred hands.

Once in the back room he smiles recognizing the plotting pair, Sam quietly and quickly tells Knuckles the plan and the bartenders part of it if he is willing to do it, the boys are not the least bit surprised when Knuckles agrees and takes the bottle. The boys listen as Knuckles takes the spiked bottle to Slashers table, "Gentlemen I have here a bonded bottle of Irish whiskey that has the smell of the peat moss and tastes of nectar of the gods, you boys are being right good customers the bottle is on the house drink up gentlemen the night is young." Slasher grabs the bottle from the bartenders hand and pulls the cork, he then inhales the scent of the spirit, "Damn boys if this ain't the real deal come boys fill your glasses and see what real drinking liquor tastes like, let's drink to the generous folks of Kingsman, we will appreciate everything we plan on taking now boys drink up." Sam tells Bruce the Doc told him it would take about 15 or 20 minutes for the knock out drug to take effect then those boys should all be lights out and I recon a bit grumpy when they come to, both men give off low chuckles and wait. One by one the outlaws fall victim to the drug and fall into a dead sleep, cannon fire would not wake them, Scraper and the Deuce come out from hiding and move quickly to the drugged men. First they remove all the outlaws guns knives and other assorted nasty weapons and have Knuckles take them away, next off comes the men's boots then their pants and shirts leaving the sleeping men only in their dirty long johns. Sam has always been a good planner he had the foresight to bring a dozen or so leather piggin strings to bind the men's ankles and wrists, with that done they get Knuckles to help and they drag them all outside and lay them in a neat row right on main street, Knuckles tells the boys he will put a pot of coffee on and goes back into the saloon the boys sit in their old wood chairs and fire up a cigars real pleased with themselves and the nights work.

Slasher opens his eyes the world spins his head feels like it is going to bust wide open it takes him a couple minutes to realized he was tied up and laying in the street in his underwear he struggles uselessly to free himself. The cocking of that damn shotgun grabs his attention, all his men are awake now angry and confused cursing uttering threats, the Deuce laughs at struggling pondscum and greets them, "A very good morning to you lads and what a lovely morning it is now you may be asking yourselves how you got into such a fix, well fellas we drugged you with MY good Irish whiskey and wrapped you up real neat so when the Ranger gets here you are no trouble for him. "A Mexican boy came in this morning says a big hard looking Ranger riding a beautiful gray horse is headed this way be here in a couple hours, MY guess it is the one they call the Stormrider. For now you are going to lay there and let good honest people see how tough you are without guns, news will travel like wildfire that the Slasher gang was laughed out of Kingsman, to humble your evil hearts before they stretch your necks." The Doc told Sam the drugged men will be very thirsty they must be given water so with Sam covering him Bruce in what some would say a bit to tough of a manner gave each prisoner his fill of water mostly on the outside.

Ranger Regret Cooper also known as the Stormrider rides slowly into Kingsman and enters main street noticing a small crowd he points his horse Storm towards the crowd see what's got folks attention, the crowd parts as he nears and he now can see Slasher and his men tied up in their underwear. After dismounting he leaves Storm ground hitched and walks over to have a closer look at his unexpected prize wondering how the holy hell this happened then he saw them. "I should have known Scraper and the Deuce this has to be your doing you boys must be getting soft I figured you would just fill them full of lead holes, damn boys this is really something now the boys will keep you 2 come with me I will buy breakfast I am hungrier than a grizzly in spring." Sam looks down the street his eyes lock on to the animal at the edge of town, it is a red fox this is strange for there are no foxes in this area and this one seemed to have a purpose he asks the Ranger about it, "everywhere I go that I go he is there, he is my spirit animal given, laugh if you like but that damn fox saved my bacon leading out a killer storm to shelter, the natives claim he is big magic." Neither of the men laughed they themselves have witnesses true magic in the wilderness, unexplained wonders and sometimes visions if you are chosen, entering the café they all ordered steak and eggs. The cookie being a old trail cook knew how men like this needed some of his strong black brew brings a big pot with cups is places them on the table then cookie gets to burning breakfast.

Cookie brings out the huge steaming steaks so big they covered the whole plate he had to bring the eggs out on separate plates a big meal for big men and they tore into it with a vengeance, the hunger now satisfied it is time for coffee talk and cigars. The Ranger passes around cigars seems he likes the same thin black cigars the boys do, but there is always a price, "Boys that is a tough bunch to handle as one man, would you men consider taking a ride back to the capital with me at deputy wages and a fine big city dinner, my old Sgt and Amigo Buck always said make sure to pick the right men to cover your back and even he would agree there is no better than Scraper and the Deuce, if your coming be ready in an hour." The Ranger pays for the meal Sam and Bruce say they will meet him at the livery in an hour they are going to grab their gear and guns and if they are lucky might find a scrap. Laughing the men separate, Bruce tells Sam he will catch up with him he is going to tell Nora he will be away a spell, Sam digging the spur in whistles the wedding march as he walks away, Bruce is doing some serios cussing now.

Nora is outside by the gate when he gets to her house, he quickly explains what has happened and that he and Sam are going to help get those coyotes back to the capital for trail and hanging and good riddance, then asks if there is anything he can fetch her back from the big city, "Bruce you big lug the only thing I want is you and Sam back safe, don't you go getting yourself killed I am not the forgiving kind Mr. Deuce, but do take care you big beautiful man." With that she gives him hug and a kiss on the check then hurries back into the house, once again Bruce stands bewildered but this time happy and he knows what he is bringing Nora back.

The boys are back in town Bruce disappointed at the lack of action on the trip did not pull his gun once not even to shoot a snake, today is the big day it is wedding day and beautiful Nora will be his forever, Sam stands beside him looking.scared and a bit overwhelmed he is not best man he is standing right next to Bruce seems Nora has a sister.

JUST DO WHAT MUST BE DONE. THIS MAY NOT
BE HAPPINESS BUT IT IS GREATNESS- GEORGE
BERNARD SHAW

KEEP TO THE CODE.

BONUS STORY

THE RETREAT UP
THE HILL BATTLE

CHAPTER 1

WAR ON THE WIND

Blue Feather the leader of the great Blackfoot nation sits in his buffalo robe blanket watching the sun setting behind the distant western mountains behind him Blue Feather enjoys this time of day most it is when feels the valley's supernatural powers and when he is closest to the valley's spirits. Many of the other tribes and people come to pray here but to Blue Feather and the Blackfoot this valley belonged to the Blackfoot, invaders will not be tolerated. The Blackfoot leader thinks at times the gods were drinking fire water making this valley, it is a beautiful green valley with high steep sandstone cliffs, the Milk river slowly winds its way all through the valley. Within all this beauty are strange rock formations they call Hoodoos, the formations look like nothing from this world as if molded by giant hands like clay, they have a fearsome look and hold great magic. The sandstone cliffs have had strange writings carved into them some of the writing so old even the eldest of his people cannot read it, Blue Feather is convinced the unknown writings are of the Sky people his Grandfather told him of when he was young, now he is at his peak of power and physical strength. A survivor of many battles known by both his people and enemies to be a brave and smart leader, the year is 1866 the place is Writing on Stone valley soon a great battle will be fought, blood will turn the grass and water red, history will call it the- Retreat Up Hill Battle.

Morning finds Blue Feather walking around the camp a Blackfoot leader does not eat until all within the camp are fed, as he walks he waves and greets people, settles a couple minor squabbles, satisfied and pleased with the day he heads back to his teepee for his breakfast, while he eats he sits in the sun enjoying its warmth enjoying the morning sounds of his camp. Breakfast finished he opens his pouch and fills his pipe with tobacco he frowns while lighting the pipe for he now sees 2 of his scouts rushing towards him, looking at their faces he does not have to be told trouble is coming and soon he tells the scouts to sit and catch their breath then tell him what they know. Raven the older of the scouts speaks for the men. "Blue Feather we come with bad news we talked with a Cree we captured and before he died he told us that the Gros Ventre, Crow and Cree are joining together and are going to attack to kill us and drive us from the valley, we scouted further and found it to be true they are gathering at Big Stone we believe there are more than 500 warriors getting ready to wipe us out we sent other scouts out to make sure we know when they come, that is all my Chief."

War will it ever end Blue Feather always preferred peace over war but this is a Blackfoot valley and after the battle it would still be a Blackfoot valley tonight he will hold a war council decide the best way to fight the enemy. His old friend Yellow Hand is a wise warrior and planner wise like the fox brave like the wolf he will plan the upcoming battle. The first thing will be to get the women and children across the river before the attack they will be safe unless the enemy breaks though Blue Feather does not want to think on it their families will have no escape and will be slaughtered and worse. He and his warriors will have to be hard an d fight strong, pushing the thought from his head he orders runners to go through the village that there will be a council at the big circle of fire this evening.

CHAPTER 2

GRANDMOTHER

Red Hawk of the Crow Chief was chosen as war leader at the council of the 3 tribes elders and warriors, Red Hawk has survived many battles but he is also is very cunning and brutal with a burning hate for the Blackfoot and will plan the attack that will wipe them out. Then and only then will the magic of the valley will be theirs, never before has there been such a gathering of warriors he will be leading over 500 warriors into battle the Blackfeet will be overwhelmed by sheer numbers, he smiles. The leaders Rabbit of the Cree and Red Moon of the Gros Ventre bands will be sub chiefs and will help direct the assault Red Hawk has already decided to send small forces down the left and right side of the valley. He then with his warriors will lead the attack with a large force right down the middle of the valley. The Blackfoot will have no cover they have to fight in the open or flee either way works for the Crow leader, when the battle is won he will cut out and eat Blue Feathers still hot and bloody heart. The attack is planned for dawn the day after tomorrow and will begin when it is shining directly into the Blackfoot's eyes, plus there are still yet more men from the plains Cree coming today to join the fight, his only concern is they do not have many horses they must attack on foot on open ground, the warriors on the sides of the valley will have the horses to bunch up the Blackfoot to make them easier to slaughter, it is a good plan and will not fail.

Blue Feather sits looking into the big fire circle, he listens now to the drums and the women chanting speaking to the night spirits the Leader feels a chill as if the soul is touched by icy fingers, but this is a good sign the ancients are with him. This night reluctantly he raises his arm stopping the music and singing it is time for war talk, Blue Feather has been thinking hard on how to defeat the enemy and has a plan, but wants to hear from his war council especially the Deceiver and life long friend Raven. Looking to his friend he asks him to speak his thoughts on the battle, Raven nods with respect to his leader and friend and addresses the council. "Once more these weaker tribes try to wipe out the great Blackfoot Nation, none has beaten us even the white eyes fear the Blackfoot, now the fools believe in combining there weak and cowardly warriors they will have us, I say this on my life this will not happen. No matter how many men they have we will defeat them and I think I know how to make them pay for their poor decisions. "We know that skunk Red Hawk will be leading the battle I know him not be clever more coyote then fox, I suspect he will put small forces to the outside and then with the main force come right for us thinking his superior numbers will destroy us. "Tomorrow we will have to move the women and children across the river and into the trees and stay there until the fight is finished, now here is my plan. "The narrowest part of the valley is at Many Gods Rock here the most experienced fighters with rifles will be like the white eye soldiers they will form a line and fire in volleys. Yellow Hand and I will take some the younger men to cover your sides, we have more horses and should have an advantage here, the rest of the warriors will be in the rocks and cover the riflemen as they retreat back to the rock where I hope to lure them in. 'We will fight moving up the rocks and cliffs this way we are above them have the high ground we will kill many, Blue

Feather will give the order when the time comes for the riflemen to fall back, that is all I have my Chief I only wish I were a wiser man", Raven sits.

The Blackfoot leader intentionally says nothing for a few minutes he wants his warriors to absorb Raven's words and see if there is any fault in them this is not about pride but survival, seeing no one was going to speak Blue Feather stands and delivers his decisions for all to hear, "I thank the gods that Raven is here to provide us with his wisdom I know of no better with a warriors mind, we will do as Raven says I will meet Red Hawk with the riflemen where the valley narrows. Raven and Yellow Hand will lead the horsemen that leaves a leader for our men in the rocks I have chosen Badger for this I know he is young but has been on 2 raids and proven himself now let the drums speak of war." The drums now have a more violent heart poundingrhythm to where it almost feels as if the ground itself was alive and moving the blood of the warriors gets hot the need for battle deep and strong, time to sharpen the scalping knives.

The moon is bright the stars sparkle like thousands of diamonds in the black of night Blue Feather has left the camp and is sitting on the round top of the tallest hoodoo this is his spirit rock where he prays and seeks guidance from the stars and the ancient one. Blue Feather chants the repeating rhythm slowly drawing him into a trance opening a bridge to other worlds, the night shimmers there is the faint sound of drums and singing a calm waves over him he feels his eyes get dim then he hears the voice. Blue feather knows this voice it is Sky Child his Grandmother who crossed over many summers ago. "Grandson it is good to see you once more my heart sings with joy and pride of the great man and leader you have become your name will be spoken over the fires long after you cross over, the spirits whisper of the upcoming battle with our long time enemies but they never reveal all. "Grandson my time is short so hear me well the fight comes in 2 suns it will be hard fought you will have to be strong and hold firm like the mountains, show no fear show the enemy the wolf that you are. I have to leave you now Grandson but once last thing the warriors look to you for courage do not fail them or you may all be wiped out, I go now."

Slowly he comes out of his trance he has never had a vision this powerful before, everything is as it was the night calm shadows everywhere from the bright moon, time to go back to camp and rest tomorrow there will be much to do. Walking back in the dark doubt begins to crawl into his heart is he strong enough, he will sleep on it things always look different in the morning sun. The morning song birds sing to a early busy camp, the women are gathering food, blankets and medicines Blue Feather has called for Spotted Pony, the warrior is past his warrior days but has a clear mind and is clever he will be the one looking over the protection of the warriors families. The old warrior was very grateful to his leader for giving him a chance to feel useful again and Blue Feather needs no longer to concern himself with the matter he needs to prepare his warriors, Blue Feather leaves the old warrior smiling knowing he has chosen wisely Spotted Pony is right he now must find, Badger, Yellow Hand and Raven to plan and prepare. Badger suggested that they get 4 of the fastest teenager runners so each group will have someone to carry messages if need be, Raven thought it a fine idea and told Badger to pick 4 and send one to each group, they are to report to the leaders as soon he has chosen them, Badger in his youth was off like a frightened deer the older men smile remembering.

CHAPTER 3

WARRIORS COLLIDE

Weasel cannot believe his luck Badger picked him over the other boys to be runner for the tribes great Leader and will be standing beside him during the battle, Weasel has not yet seen war but as all young men no matter what nation or culture war is glamorous and they are invincible. Within minutes he is at Blue Feathers side and will not leave unless to do his job as runner, just as he arrives to meet the Chief the leader begins to walk his riflemen to the spot they will fight from. After reporting to Blue Feather the young runners first job is to find some long sticks and red cloth then hurry back and meet them at the firing line. Weasel knew his Grandmother ha some red cloth and if her Chief needed it she will give it freely anything for the good of the tribe, 10 minutes later he is standing in front of Raven with the items Blue Feather wanted, Raven nods his satisfaction and tells the runner to follow him they have a job to do. Raven is very focused as he walks Weasel is curious on what they are doing, Raven stops and looks back like measuring distance with his eyes he then picks up a rock about the size of Weasels head and walks it out into the open and sets it down once away he waves to the riflemen, 2 shots are heard both are long so Raven retrieves the stone and walks further back and again puts down the stone, 2 more rifle shots show that the distance is right and this is where they will zero in. Raven orders Weasel to tie red strips of cloth to 4 of the sticks he and Weasel put up 4 small red flags across the narrow valley floor. The riflemen will all hold their fire until the enemy crosses the markers this is something he learned from watching white soldiers. Weasel is beginning to learn that there is more to battle then just fighting as a wise man once said, fail to plan, plan to fail, prepare well fight hard and victory should be yours.

The Runner stayed the rest of the day following Blue Feather the man is tireless and everywhere, Weasel runs countless errands and by the time the sun is setting the young man was wore to a frazzle but would not show it his pride strong. Finally his Chief tells him to go have his meal and try to get some rest, be back early the riflemen will be moving into position while still dark, smiling the young man runs back to his lodge. Blue Feather like his runner is bone weary but he is filled with pre battle worry and anxiety, like all soldiers past present and future his night before the scrap he will be restless and not get any sleep but this is not new to him it is always the way, tonight he will lay close to his wife the soft feel of her it always brings him comfort. The short night seems to last forever but finally it is time prepare, his wife is up making him food knowing he will need all his strength today, in a small bowl he mixes different coloured powders and bear grease to make his war paint his war colour was of course blue. Satisfied with the paint he applies his war design which is fully blue covered forehead and 3 blue lines running down each side from just below his eyes to his jawbone, it feels good to wear the paint once more. The great chief hands his wife his rifle then takes up his great spear decorated with eagle feathers and 14 black stringy enemy scalps and his knife. The long time lovers embrace then reluctantly Blue Feather tells his wife to hurry and get across the river and join the others he then steps out of his lodge, he smiles as he sees Weasel waiting for him, the young man probably spent half the night outside their tent afraid to be late. Blue Feather pats the young man on the shoulder and tells him it is time to gather the men and get into position they must be in place before the sun begins to rise, by now the camp is a flurry of activity but it is preparation not panic. Weapons are gathered up, horses made ready, men and horses in full war paint, each man is confident their medicine is strong today and they will kill many of the enemy today.

Weasel follows his leader the young man notices that Blue Feather carries no gun just his great spear and his knife, when they arrive at the rifle positions the Chief tells his men to lay flat and no man will fire until he gives the signal and to watch the distance markers. Blue Feather does not lay down like the other but stands firm as a mountain daring his enemy to kill him this Weasel begins to learn what it means to be war leader and the courage needed to lead warriors and protect all of his people. Weasel is feeling a little exposed standing beside the great man and as the sun begins to blaze it brilliant light the young runners legs nearly fail him as he sees the enemy coming towards them in a huge mass. There are to many to count, his fear grows he looks up at Blue Feather who is looking down at him. "Weasel a brave man will only die once where a coward will die many deaths, and young runner it is a good day to die, now stay close to me your work starts soon," The war cries of the enemy can now be heard some light rifle fire coming from them but to far to be accurate on the Blackfoot line there was no sound or movement just warriors waiting for the command to fire and kill the enemy. The enemy as Raven said begin to bunch up in the narrow part of the valley just as the leading warriors cross the markers Blue Feather raises his great war lance and gives a mighty war cry, the Blackfoot riflemen begin to fire. The attacking men run into a wall of hot lead accurate firing causes great numbers of the enemy to fall gaps in their lines open as men are cut down like wheat at harvest, Red Hawk is shocked at how many of his warriors were being taken out of the fight but continues to charge, he and his warriors will soon overrun the Blackfeet riflemen then the battle will turn in his favour.

Yellow Hand and Raven having the advantage of more horses rip through both enemy flanks killing many, they now are fighting their way through the enemy rear to attack from behind making them fight in 2 directions splitting their diminished forces. Weasel is frightened his mouth dry a big hand grabs his shoulder and tells him to get back to the next group of waiting warriors and tell them to get ready. The riflemen would be retreating soon and will need covering fire, he is told to run like a strong western wind, he is off and running moving faster than he ever had before his long legs and arms pumping. Smiling now to himself the doing much is easier than waiting. Blue Feather one again raises his spear with that every second rifle man rises and begins heading back to the rocks and cliffs the other firing once more to cover the retreat. The war chief now turns and leads the rest of the men back,Blackfoot arrows fly overhead and begin to pierce into the following enemy so many arrows fill the sky the sun dims. The Blackfoot now fight from the rocks and cliffs fighting as they work their way up that way always having the high ground, the fighting is now violent, close and vicious many fighting hand to hand kill or be killed, the enemy will not surrender they know how the Blackfoot treat prisoners and it ain't pretty, they like all brave warriors throughout history want a quick warriors death. Call is destiny, fate, kismet, or the gods just having their fun it seems like the 2 top dogs always find each other on the battlefield.

Red Hawk and Blue Feather see each other at the same time the Blackfoot leader drops the great spear and pulls his knife the Crow drops his rifle and pulls his blade with screams both men charge each other today will see who the better man is. The Crow is bigger and heaver than the Blackfoot and a very good knife fighter, Blue Feather is slim, fast, wang leather tough and likes to fight with cold steel. The 2 men circle each other looking for an opening the Crow draws first blood as the Blackfoot's foot slips on a loose stone with a mighty slash Red Hawk cuts his enemy across the chest a long cut but not deep blood is already soaking into Blue Feathers buckskin shirt. The Blackfoot knows it is not a serious wound but if he loses to much blood it will make him weak and at the Crow's mercy he must attack fiercely. It is all or nothing the Blackfoot uses his speed and strength and aggressively attacks the Crow blades flashing the

Crow begins to step back then with a beautiful feint the Blackfoot he gets behind the Crow and quickly sticks his knife deep into the doomed mans kidney, then quickly moves the knife cutting open the crows throat, Red Hawk is on his knees bleeding out fast but before he stops breathing Blue Feather grabs up the Crow' greasy hair and scalps him. Blue Feather retrieves his lance and holding his enemies bloody and gory scalp he screams victory. The enemy warriors seeing their leader dead know they have lost and their medicine is not strong this day in fear they flee but many are rode down by Raven and Spotted Tail and wiped out. The battle has ended except for killing the enemy wounded now time to see to the wounded, it is a great day for the Blackfoot, once more an enemy has paid dearly for underestimating the Blackfoot warriors.

Blue Feather looks over a now quiet battlefield even he is shocked by the number of enemy dead, he is proud his enemies fought and died bravely, tomorrow he will send a courier to tell the survivors that they can come collect their dead no harm will come to them, later that evening Raven tells him he and his men counted over 300 dead enemy and their losses were light more with wounds than killed. The great battle, "Retreat up the hill Battle", is fairly and decisive won by the Blackfoot.

MAY THE STARS CARRY YOUR SADNESS AWAY, MAY
THE FLOWERS FILL YOUR HEART WITH BEAUTY,
MAY HOPE FOREVERE WIPE AWAY YOUR TEARS-
CHIEF DAN GEAORGE

Authors note, although the story is fiction the battle did take place at the time and place as in the story, names were invented as there is no evidence of leaders at the time, "Writing on Stone" is a real place and can be googled, the battle scene can also seen in carving in the sandstone rock, Alberta is a place to be visited we have the mighty Rocky mountains, Badlands. Foothills, Coulees, Smashed in Head buffalo Jump, Writing on Stone and flatlands as far as the eye can see. This may not be how it was but how it should have been.

Thanks for reading

Be seeing you down the trail, Adios